# Sleep in a Ditch

He lay curled in the gutter one raw February morning outside the doors of a London East End Settlement. He might have been asleep, but he was dead.

He was a stranger to all the social workers, except that one week previously he had called on Kate Weatherley, deputy director of the Settlement, apparently to seek help from the Citizens' Advice Bureau. He had given the name of the husband she had left years ago. Coincidence? The police were understandably suspicious now that he was dead at her door.

Where was Kate's husband, and what was the connection between him and this unknown junkie? Could they be one and the same? Kate insisted not, if only because their eyes were a different colour, but there was only her word for it. And the reasons for which she had left but never divorced her husband meant that now, nearly ten years later, she had a strong financial motive for surviving him. She had to trace the husband with whom she had deliberately lost all contact. Or identify the mysterious young man.

Kate could not have foreseen the strange links this would create with a squatters' commune, nor that her enquiries would put her life at risk. Someone wanted Kate dead, but who or why proved terrifyingly uncertain, for it looked as if it must be one of those she trusted most.

MAISIE BIRMINGHAM

# Sleep in a Ditch

COLLINS, ST JAMES'S PLACE, LONDON

479030012

William Collins Sons & Co Ltd
London · Glasgow · Sydney · Auckland
Toronto · Johannesburg

2027128885

First published 1978
© Maisie Birmingham, 1978

ISBN 0 00 231747 8

Set in Baskerville
Made and printed in Great Britain by
William Collins Sons & Co Ltd, Glasgow

# CONTENTS

For Beth,
who first introduced me to Holmes and Wimsey,
for John and Muriel,
and for Margaret and Noel, Andrew and Kathryn,
Rosemary, and David,
with my love.

# SPITALFIELDS RESIDENTIAL SETTLEMENT
## GROUND FLOOR PLAN

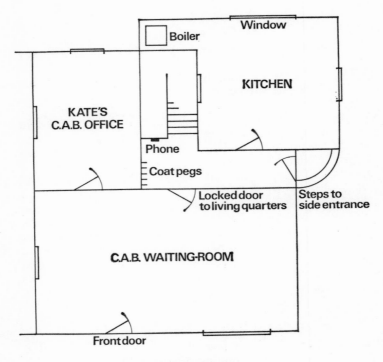

Boiler

Window

KITCHEN

KATE'S
C.A.B. OFFICE

Phone

Coat pegs

Locked door
to living quarters

Steps to
side entrance

C.A.B. WAITING-ROOM

Front door

WENTWORTH STREET

# MONDAY, 14 FEBRUARY

## I

THE WEEK BEGAN HORRIBLY. Very early on Monday morning, in the gutter immediately outside our side door, was a young man, huddled on his side as if trying to sleep. But he was dead. He was not quite a stranger to me.

We never learnt who found him first. When the night was fading, an unknown man rang the police to say there was a body outside our door. Perhaps the same man had gone through his pockets first. Certainly there was not a penny or a paper on him when the police arrived. But then they were slow. The unknown caller was not a local; he rang the City police. The police station almost opposite Liverpool Street railway station is indeed the nearest, but that is the City. We, in Spitalfields, are just outside and we all know that the City police have no authority or interest in us. The constable on duty had tried to explain this to the caller, but he was not prepared to do more and had rung off. Reluctantly the constable had himself rung the Metropolitan police station in Leman Street.

By the time the car, with four police, had driven up from Leman Street, it was already lighter. Stall-holders had started arriving, planning to get their stalls up early on what held some hope of being a fine morning. Half a dozen had turned up our little side street to see what was wrong and had decided that the man, whether drunk or dead, would be better in our house than in the gutter. They had lifted him up our two steps, propped him against our door, and pressed our bell.

I don't know how many times they had to ring before I realized that the pealing bell was not part of my dreams.

Still half asleep, I struggled into my dressing-gown, ran downstairs and opened the door just as the police car drew up.

With the supporting door gone, the body rolled over slowly until it lay face downwards in the hall. Ours is a narrow hall, really only a passage, with no room for me to get out of the way, so the man lay against my legs, and I knew at once, from the cold, or the rigidity perhaps, that he was dead. I was not shocked; it seemed just then only part of my dream and I a remote onlooker, with no part to play.

Handling such a matter was clearly standard routine for the police. Leaving one in the car and one on the pavement to take the names and addresses of the by-standers, two came up the steps and into the house, effortlessly carrying me backwards before them. One went straight to the phone in the hall, while the other manoeuvred me into the kitchen just beside us. He was calm enough to find time for courtesy.

'Good morning, ma'am. Now I wonder if Mrs Campbell would like to come down and join us at once.'

Agnes Campbell is not only the Director of our Settle-ment but our usual link with the police.

'I'm sorry. Mrs Campbell and most of the others are away this week at a conference. I'm the Deputy Director, Mrs Weatherley.'

'So you're alone in the house, Mrs Weatherley?'

'Not quite. Kevin Kershaw, one of the Residents, the newest, is still here, and we're expecting—'

'There were only the two of you in the house last night? And is the deceased known to you?'

'I suppose—I think I could—'

The sense of remoteness was fast fading. If I was still in a dream, it was one in which I was inescapably in-volved. I tried to get a grip on myself.

'Yes. I have met him once. He came as a client into our Citizens' Advice Bureau here, which I run.'

'Do you remember his name?'

I took a deep breath. The dream was becoming a nightmare. I could not move although I wanted to go out into the hall again and look at the dead man and make sure.

'He gave a false name.'

'A false name. I suppose in a place like this that's not unusual. And you don't know his real—' He broke off, thinking. He was in no hurry. 'How did you know it was false, Mrs Weatherley?'

There was a hammering in my head. I had got out of bed too quickly and too early and had run too uncaringly down two steep flights of stairs, hadn't I, Mrs Weatherley, Mrs Weatherley, Mrs Weatherley. It was more like drums than hammers.

'He said he was Ralph Weatherley—my husband.'

Into the silent room—even the drums had fallen still—came a mocking Cockney voice, raised above the murmur and shuffling outside:

'Ain't it gra-and
To be blooming well dead.'

I found I had no handkerchief and had to use my hands to push the tears off my face.

II

'It isn't Ralph who's dead. This is quite silly of me. I'm sorry. It's too early in the morning for me. I'm sorry about the man who's dead. But it's not Ralph.'

I tore a paper towel off the roller and blew my nose. The policeman was looking at me rather helplessly. His enquiries were not proving as straightforward as he had expected. He pulled one of our chairs out from the big table and handed me into it.

'Now just you sit there quietly, Mrs Weatherley. One of us will be back in a minute.' But he turned again at the door. 'You are quite certain that the deceased was not your husband?'

'Quite certain,' I said firmly.

But I was sorry he shut the door behind him as he went. I wanted to look at the dead man again—just for re-assurance. I had only seen the face when the body had rolled over into the hall, but that had been slowly and stiffly enough to give me plenty of time. I had had no doubt at all then that it was the body of my recent client. It was absurd of me to start imagining that I might have projected on to what were really unknown features a face that had been in my mind this last week. Or worse still, that what I had taken to be again the face of the impostor had this time been, in reality—I twisted away from that.

I forced myself to turn to more immediate matters. Why was Kevin not down with me by now? Agnes and the other Residents when they went away had all assumed that in any of the crises which beset our lives in Spitalfields I should at least have Kevin to help me. They had not visualized death on our doorstep nor had they imagined that at such a time Kevin would sleep peacefully—but I knew I was letting my personal unease make me unfair. Both our rooms were on the second floor, where the bell had had difficulty in waking even me, usually a light sleeper, whereas the soundness of Kevin's sleep was a household joke.

I found myself thinking sadly that in spite of all the months he had lived at the Settlement, and in spite of his apparent willingness to stammer out the secrets of his heart to any of us, Kevin was still half a stranger. I should have felt quite different if Agnes or Michael, Betty or even the playboy Tom had been here with me. Could I per-suade myself that to tell them what had happened and bring at least one of them back to the Settlement was the right thing to do? 'The right and proper thing to do,' sang a disjointed bit of my mind; I did not seem able to con-centrate this morning.

The door was flung open and Kevin, followed by a policeman, burst in. He was in an absurdly short woolly dressing-gown and his ginger hair stood out in all directions.

'Wh-why on earth didn't you call me, Kate? I'm not a h-hibernating h-hedgehog. What *do* you think you're doing? For h-heaven's sake, wh-whose breakfast are you making?'

I looked down in surprise at the boiling kettle in my hand. My mind was even more disjointed than I had realized. But there seemed no point in admitting it, and anyway, familiar company, even Kevin's, helped.

'I assumed everyone would need some tea. Get some cups, please, Kevin.'

I concentrated on how many policemen would want tea, and hunted out the sugar, which none of us take but I expected the police would, until I realized suddenly that an ambulance had arrived and was collecting the body. I hurried out into the hall just as the ambulance moved away. So I had no chance to check again on whether I had known the dead man.

'What did he die of?' I asked the policeman abruptly.

'I don't know, miss.' This was not the well-spoken sergeant who had been with me before. 'Exposure, perhaps. He was a junkie, you know, full of holes, like a sieve. Can't stand exposure, they can't. Just curl up and die. And I don't suppose no one misses them.'

'I-I do think you must be wrong there, Constable. I think a wh-whole lot of people could easily be missing a good-looking bloke like that. Don't you think so, Kate?'

'Of course. He's probably got parents and a family who'll grieve over him.'

The constable was unimpressed. 'Thankful to see the back of him,' was all he said, as he stirred three spoonfuls of sugar into his tea.

The police left soon afterwards, having drunk all the tea I had made. The sergeant, who had been with me at first, checked where we should be the rest of the morning, as one of them would want to take statements from us. He made a note of Kevin's office address, and I unlocked the door which leads from the residential part of the Settlement into the C.A.B. waiting-room, to show him where he would find me.

'At nine o'clock I'll unbolt that big front door into Wentworth Street, and lock this other one behind me of course, and then I'll be in the office opening off at the back there. See?'

I let the sergeant out and went back to Kevin in the kitchen. To do him justice, he had already put a pan on the stove and cracked two eggs into it.

'You-you like your egg cooked both sides, Kate? I thought we might as well h-have a good breakfast at once while we're h-here as go upstairs and dress first, though I know I look like a cuckoo in the nest in this dressing-gown. Do you mind?'

'It's a splendid idea.' I ignored the dressing-gown. 'I think breakfast is just what I'm needing. Yes, turned over, please.'

Perhaps I didn't really want to be alone, with time to think. Even while I was serving the police with tea, I had found myself trying to remember whether the falsely-named client had been obviously on drugs. Certainly I hadn't noticed it but perhaps I had been too busy listening to his outrageous claims. That must have been it. This must be the same man. Kevin's chatter was a relief.

'N-never a dull moment round h-here, is there? I can't think h-how anyone ever settles anywhere else after once living h-here. And they talk about living anonymously in big cities!'

'London's really only a collection of villages—no chance of anonymity at all. Look where we live—in the Tower Hamlets.'

'D-did everybody, except a newcomer like me, know the poor bloke?'

'I've no idea. I'll hear from our neighbours during the morning, I expect. They'll find excuses for coming to "have a word with me" in the C.A.B. Mrs Weinkopf will probably tell me that the first time she saw him come into the waiting-room she saw death in his face.'

I was chattering too. It saved me from thinking.

'S-so at least you know him.'

'I don't know him from Adam. He's just been into my office once, briefly.'

It was myself I was annoyed with really, not Kevin. I had not meant to tell anyone but the unavoidable police of that previous encounter. Perhaps I was annoyed with Kevin too. I had noted before that his apparent guilelessness sucks in information like a vacuum cleaner.

'Anyway, seeing he died in the street, apparently of natural causes, and it's too late for us to do anything helpful, he needn't interrupt our work,' I said rather loudly.

I got up and started to clear the table to make sure the conversation ended. But there was something about Kevin's very silence which made me go on.

'And he wasn't asking for help—even indirectly—when he did come in.'

I had not realized until I said it that among my other, more personal anxieties was professional guilt at the death of a client whom I had done nothing to help.

Kevin did his best. 'It's a t-tightrope, isn't it,' he said, 'being real friends with one's clients and yet not getting so involved that you drown with them. I expect it's lucky we're all so busy. That reminds me. I was thinking. What with all this, would you rather we dropped the idea of Jack moving in?'

'Goodness, no! It will be nice to have more people in the house. And your cousin would never find anywhere else in London at a moment's notice.'

'G-good. H-he'll be h-here this evening then. H-he's not really my cousin, you know. H-he's just the son of one of those friends of my parents that I used to call Aunt. So we pretended to be cousins. We saw a lot of each other when we were young, and solemnly promised to use each other as best men, but I h-haven't needed Jack yet. H-he's a frightfully nice bloke. I h-hope you'll like h-him, Kate. I'm sure h-he'll like you.'

I managed not to say, 'Lucky my name isn't H-helen.'
I suppose I had never before been so long on my own with
Kevin—certainly not with me in so touchy a mood. So
we parted in amity to get dressed for the day's work and
I had to face my own thoughts—and memories.

III

Perhaps there really was thunder in the air. Certainly a
sense of threat, of impending disaster, deepened as the
morning went on. Usually the C.A.B. offers me freedom
from my own worries. Other people's far worse problems
are an odd source of cheer, yet to be on top of one's job,
to believe one is coping adequately in a demanding and
worthwhile occupation, is a prime source of serenity. But
today the office was alive with memories of the dead
client—I half expected to see him every time the door
opened to admit another face—and behind him, older,
long-dead memories stirred.

Once in the office, at least I had no time to brood, nor
even to look back at the entry in the day-book I had made
a week ago. As I had expected, half a dozen locals were
already waiting in Wentworth Street when I unbolted the
big swing door into the waiting-room. They let old Sam
in first, recognizing his squatter's rights to our gas fire,
by which he spends his days, and jostled in after him, the
tone of their morning greetings lowered, like half-mast
flags, in honour of death.

"Morning, miss.'

'A dreadful thing—in the prime o' life—'

'I expect you knowed just what his problems were, miss.
Half-starved he looked, as I said to our Linny last time.'

'Too proud to claim his insurance, like some of them
are these days.'

I let them into my little office one by one. They had
all thought up some good reason for seeing me that
morning. After all, there is no lack of problems in the

condemned flats all round us—nor in the new high-rise
block. With some difficulty I kept discussion of the
morning's tragedy to a minimum. It was quite a relief
to have some real cases, with the dead man unmentioned,
but there was nothing I could do for the silly girl who was
the first stranger.

'I wonder if you can help me, miss.'

The tally of those who wonder this has grown too long
to count, but from habit, I still make a nick on the unseen
front of my desk.

'It was Uncle. He could always get money when he
needed it, when we all really needed it, when things were
really bad, like. He never told us how it come. Something
to do with insurance. But he never told us how. A real
lot of money it were sometimes. And now he's dead and
we could do with it and we keep figuring how to get it,
but it don't seem to come.'

'No. I expect it was only your uncle who could manage
it. Was it anything to do with fires?'

'Anything to do with fires, miss? No. I don't see how
it could be. There was two big fires, well, three you could
say, if you count the one when the other shop burnt down.
But you'd lose money on that, wouldn't you?'

Not many of our clients are so naïve. She must have
led a protected life. I tried to check whether there was
any real hardship.

'Me and my sister's earning quite good money, but we
thought it would be nice to have some real money like
Uncle could get. We thought perhaps you could help.'

I couldn't. She clearly thought little of me and as the
feeling was mutual I felt lower than ever by the time I
had entered her enquiry in the day-book—as innocuously
as possible—answered the third or fourth telephone call,
and admitted Mr Steel.

Jerry Steel is local but quite uninterested in corpses.
His interests are all nearer home. He is the founder and
chairman of the Spitalfields Self-Help Association, but he
has never found any difficulty in accepting our help. He

had come in today to ask if I could persuade the local housing officer to change her mind about the tenants she was going to install in the new block of flats where most of his association are housed.

'Pity to bring in somebody that isn't really going to fit in, I'm sure you'll be the first to agree, Mrs Weatherley. A really happy family we are there now, barring one or two exceptions, and you'll be the first to recognize who I mean by that.' Jerry is big and jovial with a ready flow of words that makes it quite unnecessary for me to agree or disagree most of the time. 'I've been down to the Town Hall and told them of the family we'd like there, an old couple with enough put by to be sure they can keep up the standards and fit in with the rest of us. You're the first to agree that it's essential we keep up the happy family atmosphere we've got there now, and we think a word from you down at the Town Hall would just confirm that this is the right thing.'

I've known Jerry rather too long.

'How big is the flat, Mr Steel?'

'It will probably have three bedrooms—'

'It will have to go to a family with children then. There's no question of that.'

At least Jerry knows when he is defeated and wastes no time.

'Right. Then the other family we have in mind, and I could go down and put their name forward now, if you'd just back me up, they have two children, a boy *and* a girl, so they need three rooms, as you'll be the first—'

'What's wrong with the proposed tenants, Mr Steel?'

'Nothing wrong, Mrs Weatherley, nothing wrong at all. Live and let live, that's what we always say. But neighbours have got to be suited, like in a marriage. I know, as a married woman yourself, Mrs Weatherley,'— this was hitting below the belt—'you'll agree with me there.'

'Mr Steel, the housing people have a difficult job to do and I can't try to interfere with the way they do it unless I've a really cast-iron case that they're doing the wrong thing. Just because the people they're moving in are coloured'—he did not contradict me, so I knew I'd got that right—'is not a good enough reason for letting someone else jump the queue.'

This time he wasn't taking defeat so easily.

'Now, Mrs Weatherley, you know us. Live and let live, we always say. But you'd be the first to recognize—'

Fortunately we were interrupted. A knock on the door heralded my police sergeant and a more senior officer. They eased Jerry Steel out of the room and at my invitation sat down opposite me. They were both big men. The room seemed crowded and increasingly oppressive. The new man, an inspector, took charge while the sergeant concentrated on his notebook.

'I don't expect we shall have to keep you long, Mrs Weatherley. We'd just like to take a statement about the dead man found outside your door this morning. I understand you knew him.'

'He had come once to this office. That's all I knew of him.'

'When was this? You have a record?'

'Yes. It was Monday the seventh—just a week ago.'

I started turning back the pages of the day-book but stopped when he interrupted me: 'You remember the date very well.'

'Yes. He rather upset me. I thought about him quite a lot.'

'How did he upset you?'

'As you will know, he pretended to be my husband. I think what really upset me was that there seemed something calculated about it. It wasn't just a silly joke that I would have forgotten at once. It was almost malicious.'

'And you're not used to that sort of thing in a job like this down here.' The inspector was almost sarcastic.

'We get lots of awkwardnesses—not malice.'

He let that point drop and looked at the entry in the book when I turned it round for him to see. He read it out.

'Unknown man, about thirty-five, fair straight hair, blue eyes, gave no address or name except that of Ralph Weatherley. Seemed embarrassed at my rejection of this false claim and left without presenting any problem.' The inspector looked silently at the book for a moment and then looked up at me. 'Are you sure this was not your husband, Mrs Weatherley?'

'I am quite sure.'

'Was he like your husband?'

'I suppose he was—superficially.'

'How old is your husband?'

'Thirty-four. He'll be thirty-five this year.'

'Colouring?'

'Fair-haired.'

'Straight-haired,' murmured the inspector, as if to himself. He looked at me again sharply. 'You're not living with your husband, Mrs Weatherley. How long is it since you saw him?'

'Six and a half years.' I had had time to work that out exactly this last week, since my memories had been awakened.

'Then he could have changed a lot. You can't be sure this man wasn't him.'

'Of course I can be sure.' I could hear my voice rising and deliberately brought it down—too low—it sounded unnatural to me. 'One knows one's own husband even after six years.'

'Unless he's changed. Was your husband on drugs when you were last in touch with him?'

'No. Ralph is not the sort of man who would ever go on to drugs. He is far too controlled—certain of what he is doing.'

'An emotional shock can alter a man a lot, like his wife going off.'

I let that drop into silence. I was not going to be browbeaten into telling the police all my private life. The inspector let the silence lie between us so long that murmurs from the waiting-room and calls from the market outside crept into the room, but in the end he recognized defeat.

He started again. 'Drugs can alter a man beyond recognition.'

It seemed time for me to take the offensive.

'Do you mean you have no idea who the poor man was? There must surely be someone looking for him by now. And was he really a main-liner? Did he die of exposure?'

The inspector did not shift an inch. I might not have spoken.

'How can you be sure he wasn't your husband?'

I played my ace, and only by still holding my voice low avoided a hint of triumph in this trivial, irritating little battle.

'My husband has brown eyes. Any of my friends who knew us both can confirm that. They are so unexpected under his light hair and eyebrows.'

I won no victory. The inspector looked down at the day-book still open on the desk in front of him. 'Yes. I saw you'd put that down in the book: blue eyes. The body we took away this morning has brown eyes.'

IV

Why had I put off so long facing the worst, as we call it? The truth brings its own strength. All the morning I had been avoiding the possibility that the body was Ralph's, but facing it now, my hesitations and uncertainties cleared. Perhaps I had needed time.

I was surprised how sharp was my sense of loss. I had thought that had been dealt with and drowned in my nightly tears nine years ago. There was surprising disappointment too. I had not realized until now the expectations I had built on the final settlement this coming June, only four months away, my irrational dreams, never before admitted to consciousness, of appreciation, perhaps even of gratitude.

I do not know how long the silence had lasted this time before I again became aware of the two policemen looking expectantly at me across the desk—perhaps only a few seconds.

'In that case, Inspector, I had better come to the mortuary to look at the body again and see if I can help at all with the identification. I'm sorry I misled you by thinking it was that other man who was here last Monday. I'll come over this afternoon.'

'We'd like you at once, please, Mrs Weatherley.'

'I'm sorry, there is no one to relieve me here this morning. The C.A.B. closes on Monday afternoons now, so I can be free any time you like after one.'

They protested but finally went away without me. As I saw them out through the waiting-room I was relieved to see there were only three more clients waiting. But I went back into my office alone and poured myself a glass of water from the jug I keep filled on my desk and stood by the window drinking it. The pictures chasing through my mind had nothing to do with the cold February sun on the brick houses behind us, with their dirty windows and dirtier, half-height curtains. I drank slowly, one little sip at a time. When the glass was empty I put it back on the desk, opened the door and called in the next client.

She was a stranger, in her early twenties I guessed, though she might have been older, casually dressed, short loose hair, and one of those frog-like mouths taking up most of her small face. She could lay no claim to prettiness and wore not a trace of make-up, but, if a woman can judge, she had enough sex appeal for ten. I liked her on sight—I must lack the competitive spirit.

She gave me a broad grin and held out a small, hard hand.

'Hullo! I'm Jill Metcalfe. You seemed the most hopeful person to try.' It was a nice, positive version of wondering if I could help her and rated no nick on my desk. 'Can I sit down? But I hadn't expected to find you so friendly with the law.'

I smiled back at her. 'It's all right. They're not being friendly; they're being aggressive.'

'That's good. But I bet you're coming out on top.'

We sat for a moment, weighing each other up. She was not one of our City clients, dressed as she was, nor, with her middle-class accent, was she a true local, though today she might well be living round here—like me.

I said, 'What's the problem?'—really wanting to know.

'Housing. I bet you're sick of the word. We're squatting in Romford Street. I expect you know it. It's just this side of the London Hospital. Great, lousy tenement blocks that ought to have been blown up years ago. It's five or six years since the tenants were all moved out, ready for it to be redeveloped. We've been there nearly a year now. We took it over from some friends and have got it pretty nice.'

'And you're paying your rates and everything?'

'What do you think? Rates, electricity, water, the lot. Don't you worry. We're proper, law-abiding squatters. The only people who hassle us are the London. They thought they could take over the whole giddy place, till it comes down, for their students and nurses. They've managed to grab about half the flats. But they ought to be building a proper hostel. Hospitals have the money. They don't have to squeeze out squatters.'

'But you've managed to hold on?'

'We're survivors.' She grinned irresistibly.

'So, what's the problem?'

'Sorry. I'm taking your time. Funny, it's so peaceful here with the market going full blast outside. I bet people sit here all day and pour out their life histories. Stop me if I start. Back to housing. We settled in with just the four of us, two couples. We hadn't known the other couple long but we've got on pretty well, and the squat itself is fine. There's a sitting-room, two bedrooms, kitchen and bath. Couldn't be better. Then when my boy-friend split and we let Rex move in instead, I didn't want him in my room, so he dossed down in the sitting-room. Then we picked up Art. He's a nice guy but a bit heavy. It seemed simpler if I moved into the sitting-room and let Rex and Art have the bedroom. I keep my clothes in with Sheila's.'

'Sheila's half the couple in the other bedroom?'

'Yes. Sorry if I'm making this a bit elaborate. She and Tim are a regular couple. Very steady. Anyway I moved into the sitting-room so that Rex and Art could have my bedroom. That worked all right till Lorraine moved in. We still reckon she's only a visitor. We've never taken her in as one of the co-op. But I can't say she notices the difference. It's made problems that weren't there before she came. She and Art. They never talk, to each other, I mean, if any of the rest of us are there. Funny relationship. Still, we've survived. I said we were survivors.' The grin flashed over her face again. 'But now she says her boy-friend needs to move in too. There just isn't the room, as you can see.'

'Lorraine's sharing the sitting-room with you? And where does she propose the boy-friend should sleep?'

'She says the sitting-room is big enough for all three of us, and that they won't need it long. We just don't understand her. When we said why couldn't she move in with him, she couldn't think what to say. Next day she told us he was having to give up his rooms. Why couldn't she say so at once if that really is the reason?'

'What's the boy-friend like?'

'We've never even seen him! Anyway, we scouted round and there's a group over in Bow who said they would let them have a room. They weren't very keen after all the things we'd said, but they said they'd take 'em for just two months and see how it went. And Lorraine won't hear of it! When we pushed it, she burst into tears and said she couldn't bear to leave Romford Street! It's plain crazy.'

'What do you want me to do about it? I should have thought Rex and Art and Sheila's boy-friend could have carried Lorraine and her things quietly down to Bow, without any help from me.'

'Oh! I'm glad you're tough. Most people are so sentimental. Even Sheila and Tim, who I thought were realists, can't face pushing Lorraine out. And Art just walks away if we start talking about it. But Art's got his own problems.'

She relapsed into brooding over the unknown Art's unknown problems, until I said, 'So you and Rex prove to be the only realists.'

'Oh, Rex is OK. He's tough enough, and fun with it.'

'You still haven't told me what you hope I can do.'

'Sorry. This has really got me down. Rex and I have got the other two to agree that if we can find Lorraine and her friend any sort of place of their own, instead of pushing them in with not very welcoming strangers, we'll all insist on their going.'

'Is Art in with this, and Lorraine?'

'Lorraine isn't, of course. We've just stopped talking to her about it. Anyway, we've never admitted her to the co-op. She doesn't have to be in on decisions. You have to have some agreed set-up to make a place like ours work.' She sounded defensive, but I guessed what worried her was less her rejection of pure anarchism than her rejection of Lorraine. 'And Art just walks away, if he's there in the first place. So I've come in to see if you do have any list of places you could suggest. It has to be near here, or Lorraine would manage to persuade Tim and Sheila that it wouldn't do. But it doesn't have to be anything at all special. It's the things we've done to ours that makes it nice. When we first moved in, the bog leaked, and the gas just gushed all over the place from old, leaky pipes. They've had to be disconnected. But it's really nice now.'

She smiled affectionately, thinking of it, and I seized the moment to say: 'Where have you tried so far?'

'We've tried all our usual lines. There's a lot of squatting in Hackney. Sorry. You know that, of course, and how it tends to be fearfully well-organized and semi-permanent. I don't think they could break into that. Most of our friends seemed to be stashed in Bow, which Lorraine has already said is too far east, or right over in the west. There's not much we know as central as us.'

'Have you tried any of the other advice centres round here? Or even in the City, if it has to be so central?'

'No. You're the first. Art's been saying he has some contact here. That's what made me think of you. And I've come near telling you my life history after all. Aren't I absurd?'

'I'm sure there's plenty of your life to hear yet.' But I was conscious of having let her talk more than I normally would in a straightforward enquiry like this—Jill wasn't here for counselling.

I turned firmly to housing matters and gave her a few addresses that might be of help. She had written off the Hackney squatters' associations too quickly. They are not as formal as all that and they spill into Tower Hamlets. I explained that she would have to give any potential helper information about Lorraine and her boy-friend's sources of income, but on this she seemed remarkably ill-informed.

'We've never met him, remember. And Lorraine herself is one of those people who talks about herself all the time without telling you anything. We think her boy-friend supports her. She's terribly hard up one moment and rolling the next.'

She seemed in no hurry to go, and said out of the blue, 'It's funny, you rather remind me of Sheila, the same dark good looks, not anything else. But you really leave her standing. I think you're what she'd like to look like.'

She was profuse in her thanks and not only gave me her address most willingly but a warm invitation to drop in any time I was that way.

'You never know how you'll find us, of course, but then I expect you're used to communes. Oh! I've just had a much better idea.' For the first time in the whole long interview, she struck me as embarrassed. 'If you'll come in tonight, you'll find us really tidy. It's not exactly a party, a sort of open house, with everybody bringing a bottle. Why don't you all come? There's lots of you live here, aren't there?'

'Only two of us are here at the moment. I don't know—'

'Do come if you can, as many as you can. Any time after eight. It'll be fun. And then you can suss out Lorraine —and the boy-friend, if he comes. And Art will be pleased. Be seeing you.' She gave a little wave and went, almost as though she did not want to give me time to reply.

By then it was nearly one. The pale sunlight had been replaced by a fine rain. I was beginning to feel cold and hungry. My appointment at the mortuary loomed blackly before me, blotting out any thought of parties. I was disappointed to find the other two clients had not been discouraged by the long delay, but, a little aggrieved, were still in the waiting-room. They, and their problems, and how little I or anyone could do for them, were only too well known to me.

I gave them eight minutes each and as I showed the last one out, I helped old Sam to his feet, from where he sat endlessly dozing by the gas fire.

'Come on, Sam. You know we shut at one on Mondays now. You go and try the public library. On a miserable day like this, perhaps they'll let you in.'

But he'd smell worse than ever once he'd been in the rain, so they probably wouldn't.

I bolted the outside door, locked my own inner office, turned off the fire and let myself through the communicating door into the residential part of the Settlement. In the empty house, as I ate a quick lunch and got ready for the police car which was to collect me at two, I tried to think if there were any other help I could give Jill Metcalfe's overcrowded ark, but the faces of my husband, Ralph, and the impostor, Ralph, and the dead man, who might be one or the other or neither, had again taken over my mind.

V

The police not only collected me—dead on time—they delivered me back to the house, some two hours later. I had spent only a few minutes at the mortuary and the rest at the station, making a statement. I wondered, on the short drive back, why I felt so drained. I should have been elated: the body was not Ralph's.

Mortuaries are not my favourite places, but I have visited them before and I can take them. The ones I know are run efficiently and hygienically. The corpses I have had to see have been of old people, sick, unhappy and invariably lonely, or it is not I who would have been identifying the body. I could not grieve for their deaths— only for their lives, which had become so thin and empty. Today's body had been different, comparatively young, and the syringe marks, so far as I could judge, not nearly so plentiful as the constable had suggested: a junkie, but perhaps not for very long and even perhaps not irredeemably so—if he had lived.

I was given no time to grieve. Perhaps that was just as well: grief might have been taken as proof that this was no stranger to me. I was there to recognize and if possible identify, but I was not good at it. I know my friends— don't we all?—by their spirits, their movements and voices. I don't think I look at them much. But clients I do look at, to learn all I can about them, and particularly to judge whether the problem they are presenting to me is the real one or just a façade, conscious or unconscious. So although the rigid, dead body was in many ways radically different from the man, full of nervous, jerky energy, who had come to the advice bureau the previous week, I would still have been prepared to identify the thin, rather fine features, the discontented mouth, the fairly long, straight, light hair, if the police had not insisted on pulling up an eyelid to show the dark brown eye. So it was not my client, lying dead in the cold white room.

Nor was it Ralph, thank God.

The police, when they took my statement, back at the police station, found this extraordinarily hard to accept. And yet why should they expect it to be Ralph? The only link was the blue-eyed client, who had claimed to be him. And he was not dead either. But the police were not interested in logic or probabilities. Not unnaturally, they wanted an identification, and the only one on the horizon was apparently that of Ralph Weatherley.

'After six years, Mrs Weatherley, you can't be sure.'

I was sure. I would know Ralph's mouth and hands however much he changed.

They wanted to know, of course, just what the client had said. I could not recall exactly, though I had been trying to for the last week. He had made me angry and this had distorted and suppressed my memory.

He had kept asking from various angles if I did not remember him, recognize him, feel glad to see him. He had called me Kit; no one but Ralph has ever done that. The police rightly picked on this, asking who else would have known this.

'All our mutual friends—dozens of them.'

What I could remember quite clearly was that it was only when I had at last tried to make an entry in the day-book, as a beginning to discovering his reason for coming to the advice bureau, and had asked his name, that he had said:

'I would never have believed that you could forget like that: Ralph Arthur Weatherley. Does it come back to you now, Kit?'

And I had said: 'You're talking absolute nonsense. You'd better go at once, before I call the police'— a most unprofessional remark, which I now much regretted. The police only regretted that I had not acted on it.

I had refused to tell them anything about my marriage and the reasons for our separation. I was not proud of any of it. I had found myself remembering a university convocation in Ghana, when I was a little girl. My father had taken me to see the chiefs in the bright, hot sunlight, dressed in their brilliant cloths, under their huge, colourful umbrellas, but what had stuck in my mind were the opening words of the university college's principal. To an assembly of incredulous new graduates, looking forward to enjoying at last the wealth towards which they had laboured, he had said: 'I have only one thing to say to you: never do anything for money.' I smiled wryly at the recognition that my marriage, and its comatose continuation these last nine years, had been primarily for money.

'What are you laughing at?'

But how could I explain that thought to the police? It would have made them more suspicious of me than they were already.

I said goodbye to them at our door and with relief let myself into what I knew would still be a peacefully empty house.

In the kitchen beside me, a man was singing, not loudly but clearly, in a deep voice I did not know:

'I'll tell you why I'm a hobo,
Why I sleep in a ditch:
It isn't that I'm lazy, no,
I just don't want to be rich.'

## VI

'A man after my own heart,' I said, as I walked into the kitchen.

He had been washing up at the sink, which is under the window, so when he turned, I could not see him clearly. But I heard the laughter in his voice.

'You don't want to be rich either? That's splendid. Let's be hobos together.'

'But I don't like sleeping in ditches.' I pushed away from me the memory of the man who had been found in our gutter that morning.

I switched on the light. This was a big man, perhaps not as tall as Michael, who is the tallest of our Residents, yet bigger, his features too large and mobile for good looks and his eyes too relentless—or so it seemed, as he too looked at me.

'It's a risk you have to take,' he said, and he seemed for a moment to be talking of something more serious—and more personal—than ditches. But he went on: 'You can't be sure of avoiding it unless you opt for riches, after all. Which do you choose? The risk of ditches or the risk of wealth?'

I dodged the question. I do not open my heart to strangers.

'I'm Kate Weatherley. I presume you're Jack Winters.'

His handclasp was warm and firm, and he accepted easily the change of topic.

'Kevin brought me in for a quick late lunch, and then had to shoot back to the office. It's good of you to take me in.'

'Saved from the ditch this time.'

'Quite undeservedly. I really am grateful and you must let me know what I can do to help while I'm here. I've been trying to answer your non-stop phone but I'm not very useful on that yet. I'll get some tea now. That's more straightforward.'

I hung my coat in the hall and washed in the first-floor's bathroom. When I went back into the kitchen, he had two cups of tea on the table, and two chairs in front of the electric fire.

'You don't take sugar,' he said, still standing, in case I did want it after all. But it was not a question, any more than his next remark: 'You've had a rotten day.'

'Yes. Kevin told you about the body this morning? I've been with the police on and off ever since. Have they been bothering Kevin too? No? That's interesting. It doesn't do to be the first on the scene, nor to think you recognize a body and get it wrong.'

'Did you?'

'I must have. The man I thought it was had blue eyes, and the dead man has brown eyes.'

'You're sure about the first man? You knew him well?'

'I didn't know him at all, but he came into my office and pretended he was my long-absent husband. There were resemblances, but one of the differences was that Ralph has brown eyes, so I couldn't help noticing that this man's were blue, light blue.'

'What do the police make of that?'

'Oh! They'd like me to admit that either the impostor or the dead man, or preferably both, is Ralph. They'd settle for the dead man as that would solve their identification problem, and then they'd cheerfully forget all about my client.'

'Extraordinary! Three somewhat similar men—'

'No. It's only two, very alike—like identical twins, except for the colour of their eyes. My husband doesn't come into it at all. It's infuriating that the police keep trying to drag him in.'

He weighed that up and came down against me. 'You can't blame them for that. The first man claimed to be your husband and the second, only distinguishable by his eyes, dropped dead at your doorstep. What did he die of? Kevin didn't know.'

'They haven't done the post-mortem yet. I suppose it may have been exposure. I hope it proves not to be—at our own door, with two of us inside.'

Some strain must have been shown, because it was he who changed the subject this time. He looked at me hard for longer than one expects and then said:

'Let's have a break. You go and rest. When Kevin comes in, we'll pull some supper together and call you down.'

'We're all invited to a party at an unknown but not far distant commune, any time after eight. It's very unprofessional to accept invitations from clients—it's someone who came to the office that's invited us—but I'm not counselling the girl, just giving her a few addresses. Kevin will want to go. He's anxious to get to know more of the people round us. What about you? Will you come?'

'I will. But you get some rest first. We won't want you dragging us home early from the party.'

'Do I look as bad as that?'

But I went upstairs, kicked off my shoes, lay on the bed with the eiderdown over me and fell fast asleep. If I dreamt, the dreams went as unnoticeably as they came.

VII

The three of us, Jack, Kevin and I, went to the party together, in remarkably good spirits.

Kevin, quite excited, had woken me with some soup and toast on a tray. 'Th-they're bound to give us things to eat there. No point in stuffing ourselves h-here. I wouldn't let Jack cook anything. H-how nice they asked us all. It's a splendid first evening for Jack.'

I walked between them, holding up the long, warm skirt I had put on—not all the communes I know are warm enough for my taste. The sky had cleared again, but a very young moon gave no help in finding our way among the little dark streets lying south of the Whitechapel Road—part of a much older London than the wide Commercial Road that now cuts through them like a fire-break.

Talking, we somehow missed Romford Street, came up against the sprawling hulk of the London Hospital, and had to turn back; but just before half past eight the old tenement blocks we were looking for lowered blackly over us. By the light of Kevin's torch, we found the entrance labelled 1 to 18.

'A s-smelly old street,' said Kevin as we felt our way up the dark, open stairs.

'Good position,' said Jack. 'One minute from Whitechapel tube station. When you throw me out, I'll find a squat here.'

'You won't. Even long-standing squatters can't find any empty flats round here. Didn't I tell you that that's exactly our Jill's problem—overcrowding in the commune?'

'Jill will take me in, you see. Didn't you say she's without a current boy-friend?'

'She doesn't acknowledge one, but I'm a bit uncertain of Rex's placing. I have an impression he's coming up fast.'

'On the inside too.' Jack managed to sound as gloomy as if he had been an aspiring suitor of Jill's for years past. He did nothing by halves.

The door of No. 14, on the fifth floor, flew open as we knocked. We might just as well have said 'Sesame', I thought, as the light streamed out of the flat across the dark stairway, waves of warmth too—my warm skirt would be quite unnecessary—and waves of sound. I could not recognize the modern record playing quietly in the background, but it did not drown the voices and laughter on every side.

None of us knew the tall, dark girl who had opened the door, but she took us entirely for granted.

'Let's get this door shut, before the old bag opposite starts kicking up. Dump your bottles in the kitchen'—we had acquired these necessary entry permits on the way—'and get yourselves something to drink. And there's pegs out there, if you want to take off anything. We seem to have overdone the heat tonight.' So this was presumably Sheila, deliberately letting her voice carry through the half-open door of the dark flat opposite, and at the same time too shy to meet my eyes. But of course it could be Lorraine, playing hostess too, as seemed not improbable from what Jill had said of her.

The door opened straight into the sitting-room, and the two adjoining bedrooms had been thrown into the party area, their doors flung wide. Coloured paper over the lights made unexpected changes to our complexions and clothes. The company, not very large as yet, sat on beds, or cushions on the floor. It was much the same as thousands of parties taking place every day, but Jill had been right about their having made the flat nice—I especially appreciated the way they had fitted up the little kitchen—and not all parties so successfully avoid a rather forced gaiety. The atmosphere was happy and relaxed—or so I thought the first part of the evening.

As we threaded our way to the kitchen we were intercepted by a slim, lightly bearded young man, who rose effortlessly from somewhere at our feet, to greet us rather formally.

'You've come over from Spitalfields? That's really nice. I hope you found us without too much hassle. I'm Rex. Let's see where Jill's got to.'

He produced her without difficulty, smiled at us engagingly, murmured, 'Be seeing you,' and sank again to his group of friends on the floor—a competent young man. I wondered fleetingly how he and Jack would rank as rival suitors—Jack struck me as competent too.

Jill, having seen we all had drinks and a modicum of food—I hoped Kevin would not be disappointed—distributed us round the party. I was given to a small, somewhat overdressed girl in her mid-twenties. She was a blonde—natural, I thought—and either I had seen her before or she was very like someone I knew, but I could not place her. She detached herself readily from two young men, lying at her feet side by side—like sardines still with heads—and greeted me most warmly.

'You're Mrs Weatherley, Kate Weatherley? That's lovely. I'm Lorraine. We've been looking forward ever so much to meeting you and your friends. You're rather like us, aren't you? You live in a sort of commune too. But you do much more than us for other people, don't you? Clubs and C.A.B.s. We keep trying. We organize protests and things. Jeff here'—she caught one of the two sardines, who had both risen quickly and appeared to be making their escape—'he runs the food co-op in Bethnal Green Road.'

'Is that still going? That's really constructive,' I said

with genuine enthusiasm. 'Are the local people using it now? I've told some of my clients who live out there about it—a splendid way to keep down costs.'

'Not as many as we'd hoped. It's still mostly just us freaks. And as I see it, it's too much work, always done by the same people, to be worth it for that.'

'Well, it must at least save you and your friends a lot of money.'

'Money's not our problem.'

'What is?'

'Relationships. But that's every—'

'Oh! I don't agree with you, Jeff.' Lorraine was as heated as he was cool. 'For some of us relationships are so easy. The only thing that makes them difficult and complicated is not having enough money to go round, so people start pushing and cheating to get their share, and then it spoils things.'

But Jeff was clearly bored with Lorraine. 'We all know your views on money, Lorraine: money makes the world go round. Come and meet some of the others, Mrs Weatherley.'

'You're not going to take her away, Jeff. I've only just met her.'

Seeing Jill had particularly hoped that I would get to know Lorraine, I had to agree with her. I should know better than to confuse my job with my social life. Jeff walked off with a shrug.

'Point out people I'll be meeting, Lorraine, will you? —and their relationships to each other. I don't want to keep putting my foot in it.' I could think of no less in-direct way of discovering whether her boy-friend was there too.

She did not point them out; she took me round the room introducing everyone in turn to me. As I had expected, she took it for granted that she was one of the hostesses, but I preferred Jill in the role. Lorraine was not prepared to leave me with any of the guests, however anxious they were to detain me—and some of them were most pressing.

They appeared to be from all 'walks of life', as one used to say. Today they all walked in the squalid and derelict Tower Hamlets, some for the company of their friends, but most for the sake of a roof, half a room in a grossly overcrowded metropolis.

I had been right as to which was Sheila, and now I was introduced to her Tim, a tall, thin man, with a long, thin face, like an El Greco painting, and some years older than Sheila. He was busy in the kitchen with Jill—it appeared we were to have a meal after all. No one showed any signs of being Lorraine's boy-friend and no one was introduced as Art. Some of the later guests I knew slightly already, but this group tended to be younger than our Settlement Residents, and today those in their twenties and those in their thirties are of different generations.

Kevin appeared to be in his element. I had not realized he enjoyed female company so much—perhaps I had been taking his undisguised interest in me too seriously. He was entertaining two pretty young things with one of the tales of disaster which are a staple of his conversation. 'I-I said to h-her, "I don't think we've met," and she said, "Only when you came to my h-house for lunch last week." It turned out she was my tutor's wife, and she was absolutely furious. But she was dressed up like a parakeet that evening. H-how could I be expected to recognize h-her?'

He tried to draw me in, but Lorraine would have none of it and led me on. Jack was more successful. He concentrated on Lorraine—he might have known her for years—insisted on her joining the largely male group with whom he was talking, and that brought me in too. They were discussing with animation the distribution of the world's wealth.

'You have experience of the Third World, Kate.' Jack had wasted no time in discovering my background. 'What do you think about aid? Jeff here thinks it's nothing but a corrupting means of destroying the noble savage.'

'Hi! I said nothing about—'

'Hand-outs are one thing'—I was so glad to join a

serious conversation that I came in rather heavily—
'though necessary perhaps in famines. But aid in building
up productivity, that's surely essential if the gap isn't to
grow bigger and bigger—and we all know how dangerous
that is.'

'I don't.' Lorraine was not a woman to be left out,
whatever the subject. 'And look at all the poor people
here. They ought to be helped before we start sending—'

We were interrupted by the phone. That's the only
squat I know that has one. I wonder how they managed it.
Rex, who was on the edge of our group, leant over, recovered the phone from under a cushion, and answered it,
while those immediately around gave him the advantage
of their silence.

'Hullo—' he gave the number and went smoothly on—
'this is an answering service. Please give your name and
start recording your message: now! . . . Jacob! Fantastic!
Get round here at once, man . . . Why not? . . . Oh, cut it
. . . You don't know what you're missing. One of Tim's
most souped-up casseroles. *And* garlic bread . . . Of course
there'll be none left tomorrow . . . You mean the people?
There'll still be bodies all over the place, but some are
wage slaves and work on weekdays . . . We'll see you then,
if we're not dead. Just one thing, man: Art isn't with you?
. . . You've not seen him . . . Right. Forget it.'

That was when I first noticed unease in that happy
party.

Lorraine got to her feet with a sudden air of bad
temper. 'You are an idiot, Rex. Just forget about Art.
He'll turn up when he wants to.'

'How do you know, when you never speak to him?' For
all the content of his words, Rex's tone was as smooth as
ever. 'It was Art who particularly wanted this party and
particularly wanted these guests.' He gave me his pleasant
smile.

But Lorraine pulled me away. 'You haven't met everyone yet.' At least Jack was still in the group. I hoped he
would pursue the subject. It had odd undertones.

I had no chance to pursue anything. The party warmed up—in every sense. More guests arrived, to be greeted with whoops of delight by the increasingly uninhibited company, and to be introduced to me, one after another, by Lorraine. She was so tenacious that I began to speculate whether she would let go of me, as ticks do, if touched by a lighted cigarette. Perhaps I was growing uninhibited too, in thought at least.

The music was turned up so that a few zealots could dance, mostly the dreary, subdued versions of African dancing, which the young in Europe and America affect. But one girl I could have watched all night. She spun and rose and fell, her movements part of the music's rhythm, her partner, Tim, an unexpectedly able but unimportant foil, with his long, thin limbs somehow reminiscent of a fast-moving spider. I wondered for a moment if the swirling dancer could be Sheila, but she was watching rather tight-lipped from one side. Only when the music stopped, and the dancer collapsed, gasping and laughing, on to the nearest cushion, did I realize I had been watching Jill.

She recovered quickly and went back to the kitchen with Tim, while Rex put on another record. I wanted to congratulate her and followed in time to hear Tim say:

'He's still not here. He's a creep, when we had the party on a damned Monday, just to please him.'

'The party's going splendidly.' Lorraine was still at my shoulder.

Jill supported her. 'Everyone seems happy. Let's have supper now, Tim, and then we can get out of this kitchen and forget it.'

So we ate, without troubling to turn the music down again. I was getting a headache. I can't stand the smell of hemp and I was sick of Lorraine. There had been a particularly tiresome few minutes when I was standing beside Sheila, refusing her offer of more food, and one of the men in the group beside us had commented on the resemblance between Sheila and me. Sheila had seemed oddly displeased, but it was Lorraine who had flatly contradicted any idea of a resemblance, had canvassed support from all the other men and had hardly succeeded in keeping her temper when each man in turn agreed with the first. She covered her annoyance by pretending they were insulting my looks, which inevitably resulted in her insulting Sheila's, but her only consistent motive, I decided, was to keep attention on herself.

To my relief, not very long afterwards, she was summoned by Sheila to what appeared to be an impromptu house meeting in the kitchen.

With a sense of freedom, I looked round the crowded room, in which a few couples had started dancing again, and caught Jack's eye. He threaded his way across to me and took my empty coffee-cup.

'Ready to go home, Kate?'

'Too much. Do you mind? Where's Kevin? Neither of you need come yet if you want to stay.'

He only laughed in answer to that, and said, 'I'll find Kevin, while you're getting your coat.'

That was on a peg in the tiny hall off which the kitchen and bathroom opened. Half a dozen other coats were by now above it on the same peg, and struggling to retrieve it, I listened unavoidably to the discussion in the kitchen.

'—absurd to make a public fuss, if you ask me.'

'But we're not asking you, Lorraine.' That, of course, was Rex.

'Still, she has a point.' That must be Tim. His hearty, almost jovial voice seemed so unsuited to his thin frame that I found him hard to recognize, but it was the same voice that had been cursing the missing Art. 'The fuzz are not our favourite form of life and enquiries might not do Art any good.'

'It's the hospitals we'd ask. He's never, never stayed away more than one night before.' Jill sounded unexpectedly like a worried mother. 'I wouldn't take much notice even then, if it weren't for this party that he's been so keen on. He doesn't know, of course, that I'd managed to get the Spitalfields crowd round, but I had promised I'd try, and now it's so ridiculous, none of us with any idea—'

She stopped so abruptly that I turned my head. Jack was coming into the little hall, observed, as it seemed I had not been. He helped me with the coats and we turned to the kitchen as Kevin joined us. Rex, unruffled as ever, had stepped forward.

'Must you go already? That's really sad. The party'll go on for hours yet, but if you all have to be up in the morning—'

'That's the trouble,' I agreed. 'It's been really good to be here. It was very nice of you to invite us. Thank you, Jill.'

'I-It's been a marvellous party. I h-have enjoyed myself immensely. Thank you all very much. Do ask us again.'

Jack's thanks came last. 'Thank you very much. I appreciate your having invited me. I have learnt a lot. But I am most disappointed not to have met Art. I only hope it is not too late now. Good night.'

The sitting-room, as we walked round the dancers and stumbled over the supine smokers, was still so noisy that we could not tell how long the silence lasted in the kitchen.


## VIII

Though the streets were as dark as ever, it was easy to find our way home. We went quickly into the brightly lit Whitechapel Road, where two pathetic pros tried to join us—after all, we had one extra man. We did not need to stay there. We cut through the bombed sites and narrow alleys on the north, which are as ill-lit as those on the south, but more familiar to Kevin and me.

We were not in the cheerful, comradely spirits in which we had set out. We walked in silence at first, even Kevin silent, until I said:

'Jack, why on earth did you have to end by saying that?

Do you know Art?'

'Of course not.'

'Why of course not? I've known some of those people much longer than I've known you—or even Kevin. For all I know, you're the contact Art spoke of, and it's you—'

'When did Art speak of a contact?'

'I've no idea. Jill said this morning'—was it only this morning? it seemed very far distant—'that Art claims some contact with us.'

We walked on in silence, and it was Kevin who took my arm when I stumbled on the broken pavings. After a time Jack spoke again.

'How much do you know about Art?'

I answered slowly, disinterring the scraps I knew.

'He's been living there longer than Lorraine, but not as long as the others, and they've only been there a year. He shares one of the bedrooms with Rex. He and Lorraine don't talk to each other—not in front of the others anyway. He was very keen on having this party tonight, and for some unknown reason—unknown to the rest of them, not just unknown to us—he wanted us there.'

'Nothing else?'

'Only the things you all know. None of them have any idea where he is tonight. He's never before been away more than one night. Oh! That must mean he was out last night too. Jill has rather maternal feelings about him. He has problems, she says.'

'I'll say he has.'

'You do know him, Jack! What do you know about him?'

'Only what I learnt tonight.' He was speaking as slowly as I had done. 'He's an addict, not very deep in yet, I gather. They've been trying to help him. He's about our age, medium build, thin—users get that way—fair, straight hair, longish. Mean anything?'

I did not even trouble to answer. It was Kevin who said, 'Wh-what colour are his eyes?' No one answered that.

We were almost home. When we were inside, Kevin turned on the electric fire in the kitchen—there was a chill in the empty house—and put a kettle on the stove. Jack helped me off with my coat, and, for no obvious reason, came through with me into my office, where I looked in the day-book for the telephone number Jill had given me at the same time as her address. I locked everything again behind us, picked up the phone in our narrow hall and dialled the number. It rang three times before Rex's voice came over the line:

'Hullo. This is an answering service. Please give your name and start record—'

'Rex. This is Kate Weatherley. Has Art come in yet? . . . I don't want to be alarmist. I don't know if you've heard there was a man picked up dead outside here this morning.' Music and laughter came down the phone; the party was still in full swing. 'He was in his thirties, fair, straight, longish hair. He had syringe marks. I thought perhaps one of you might want to check at the mortuary. If you told the police, at Leman Street, that you'd been told he had some resemblance to your lodger, you wouldn't have to make any fuss about Art being missing.'

'No. Thank you. I guess we'll do that—in the morning.' Rex's voice was lacking its characteristic assurance, but he pulled it up quickly. 'Thank you very much for ringing. That was really kind. Thank you.'

There was a loud burst of laughter from somewhere in the background, as I said, 'I hope it's a false alarm. Good night,' and hung up.

'Y-you didn't ask the colour of h-his eyes.'

'No.'

Jack and I drank our tea in silence, but Kevin chattered on.

'Th-they're nice people, aren't they? Isn't Jill terrific? I do h-hope Rex manages not to say anything tonight. It would be a shame to break it up, with everyone enjoying themselves. Wouldn't it be marvellous if Art just walked in on them? There'd still be things to explain, of course, but I do h-hope that's what h-happens.'

Jack said, 'Someone's dead, whether it's Art or not.'

We found we had stopped wanting to talk to each other. We added more milk to our tea, so that we could gulp it down quickly, and went silently to our cold rooms.

# TUESDAY, 15 FEBRUARY

## I

I HEARD THE RAIN before I fully woke, even through the thick curtains with which I try to keep out the light and the noises of the market stalls going up. Our Cockney stall-holders are not quiet people and their voices carry effortlessly up to my open window, on the second floor where I sleep—but I sleep badly in the mornings. Apart from the cheerless weather, Tuesday did not start too badly.

As I dressed, I wondered whether I ought to make any telephone report to Agnes. I no longer much wanted to. Two men in the house felt surprisingly more supportive than one. I was only concerned whether Agnes would feel she should have been told. I decided there was far too little to tell.

Going downstairs I could hear Jack and Kevin already in the kitchen. A verse of Jack's favourite song floated up to me.

> 'Oh, I could travel Pullman,
> But me trousers are so thin,
> The plush they put on the Pullman seats
> Would tickle me sensitive skin.
> Tiddle-ee, umpty, umpty, umpty, um,
> Tiddle-ee, iddle-ee, ee.'

I did not know whether the meaningless final jingle, sung just as I went into the kitchen, was to replace an accompaniment or was inserted in an old-fashioned effort to save me from some embarrassing words.

They had breakfast ready on the table and I joined them.

'Good morning. You've managed to get Kevin up earlier than usual, Jack.' Kevin rarely allows himself time to eat breakfast at all.

'I'm an early bird. So are the police. They've been on the phone already. They didn't seem to mind who they spoke to. The cause of death was a massive overdose of heroin. They reckon it could not have been accidental.'

I stopped with the teapot in mid-air: 'You mean it was intentional? He really did mean to kill himself? He didn't just die of exposure outside our door, waiting for one of us to let him in?' But my thoughts overtook my sense of relief. 'He might still have been hoping someone would come. People so often take overdoses not really meaning to die.'

'Not this amount. Not someone who uses it and knows what he's doing.'

'No. That must be right. I wonder why here. Did they say if they'd found out who he was yet, Jack?'

'I gather not.'

Well, that was their job, not mine.

'I-I'll go out through the waiting-room and leave the outside door open, shall I, Kate? It's h-horrible weather for poor old Sam to be standing about outside, waiting for the door to open at exactly nine.'

Kevin's one of the kindest people I know, I thought, and wondered guiltily if I had been letting personal worries interfere with the care of my clients. There were not many today in the steadily dripping rain. I even had gaps when I could give time to my filing—or my memories. In the waiting-room old Sam steamed over the gas fire so noisomely that about eleven, when I sometimes give myself ten minutes' break for coffee, I locked my inner office, pulled on a macintosh, and ran up the road to the flower stall to buy something sweet-smelling.

'Like a medieval judge,' said Jack, when I explained their purpose to him in the kitchen. He had coffee ready for me and went on, 'I was wondering'—a more tentative opening than I had heard from him yet—'whether you can only use fully trained workers in your C.A.B. My sociology might be some substitute.' I had not known that he had any sociology: Kevin gives little away, about others as well as himself. 'I don't expect to be busy while I'm in London and perhaps I could relieve you sometimes.'

I have needed someone else to help me on the job ever since Robin went, so this seemed an excellent idea. I accepted gratefully. I could not turn him loose on my clients until I knew more about him and his qualifications, but I could use a slack day to start showing him the lay-out. In the waiting-room as we went through were three clients who had come in the few minutes I had been out, so I took Jack through to the office and sat him at a little table in the corner, out of sight of clients once they were facing me across my desk.

'Most of them won't mind your being here, if you just sit quietly making notes, or pretending to make notes, from some of these reference books that you'll be wanting to look at anyway. If they do mind, they'll tell me.'

Coming through the waiting-room, I had been pre-occupied with Jack, and had not noticed that one of the waiting clients was Wendy Donovan. She came in first, in far too emotional a state to mind Jack; she probably welcomed an enlarged audience. We all like Wendy. She's an exceptionally imaginative as well as devoted mother, and none of us, not even Sean, her bus-driver husband, finds it too difficult to put up with her dramatic scenes. Today, she burst into tears as she came into the office. The tears ran down her face and joined the raindrops already there. She was indifferent to both.

'Mrs Weatherley, not even you can do anything to help me today. I've won the pools. It will ruin us all. How can we possibly bring up good children with all that money just poured in on us?' She swung round to include Jack in her questions—he was staring at her fascinated and making no attempt to look at any reference books. 'Why should they listen to me and Sean any more, or do any more work at school, or ever go to church? We've tried so hard to bring them up right. And we'll have to leave our little flat, that we've all been so fond of'—the Council would have enjoyed that, after the Donovans' endless complaints—'and all our friends and go and live in some enormous house—'

'How much money is it, Mrs Donovan?'

'I don't know yet. I just know that I got every single one right. I mostly fill them in and Sean puts in the postal order. There can't be many people got every one right, so it's bound to be a lot.'

'Why do you fill them in, Mrs Donovan?' As a trainee, Jack was meant to be seen as little as possible and not heard at all, but I could not mind, with Wendy so deliberately including him in the whole conversation. His question certainly stopped her flow of tears. She looked at him in astonishment:

'Why, it's fun like, planning what you'll do with the money.'

'Planning what you'll do with the money.' Jack held her to it, but Wendy is nobody's fool.

'Not *this* sort of money.' She was quite scornful. 'It's when you see something you'd like to buy the kiddies and there's just no way of doing it, you say to yourself: "Perhaps next week, I'll win the pools, and then I'll come back and buy it." It makes you feel not poor any more. But you only want a bit of money, not like this, not so you've got to be different people.' The tears started running down her face again. 'We want to go on being the same people, with just a bit more money.'

'Could you keep only some of the money'—it was the best I could do on the spur of the moment—'just to buy the things you know you want, without changing your whole life-style?'

'No. We'd never manage to do that, not once the money came.' Wendy is a realist all right, for all the drama. She stood up. 'I'd best be going now. I don't want to take up your time, and you busy with a student'—to me Jack looked over thirty, as I am, and quite unlike a student—'and there's nothing you can do for us. I just wanted to tell you. I knew you'd want to know.'

'That was very nice of you, Mrs Donovan. Of course I'm glad to know at once. Thank you for coming. When you know how much it is, come in and see me again, and we can get someone to advise you on how to invest it, so it's there for when perhaps the children need it later, instead of your finding in a few months that you've spent it on all sorts of things you don't really want.'

'I'll come and tell you, but I don't think we'll invest it. That way it'll only get more, won't it? More and more, and soon we won't be thinking of anything else.' She sniffed back some of her tears and waved me back when I wanted to see her out. 'You're the first person I've told, bar the neighbours. Even Sean doesn't know yet. He's on early this week. I don't know how I'll tell him, and it was me that filled them in.'

When he had closed the door behind her, Jack said: 'Do all your clients feel you're their nearest friend, Kate?'

'Wendy Donovan is an old friend. She lives just round the back, and when Maggie had to be away—you haven't met our Maggie, yet, have you?—Wendy came in instead and kept the house spotless for us, in spite of her own job and family. She's a marvellous person.'

'Obviously. To recognize straight off what a disaster has hit them—'

The client waiting outside grew impatient and knocked on the door, pushed it wide open and came straight in—not the client after all but the police. It was the same inspector that had seen me yesterday but with a different constable, a local whom I knew slightly. I invited them in and introduced Jack: 'A cousin of Mr Kershaw's—' what I have first been told sticks, even when I have later learnt that it's wrong. I corrected myself quickly: 'No, not exactly a cousin, a very old friend.' Jack left me to struggle unaided.

The inspector, having checked that Jack had not been in the house on Sunday night, showed no further interest in him and turned back to me.

'Mr Mayhew and Mr Stayner, whom I understand you

know, Mrs Weatherley—' my blank face prompted him to look at his notebook and add, 'Mr Rex Mayhew and Mr Timothy Stayner, squatting in Romford Street'—I nodded—'they came with us to the mortuary this morning and they both identify the body found at your door yesterday as someone who had been squatting there with them. They knew him as Art.'

He paused for me to comment, but there was nothing I wanted to say, so he went on, 'Some weeks back he had told Mr Mayhew that his full name was Ralph Arthur Weatherley.' The misuse of the name shocked me less now—I was growing used to it. 'What was your husband's full name, Mrs Weatherley?'

'Ralph Arthur Weatherley. If Art could have been the man who came here last week, he seems to have been falsely using my husband's name at his home as well as here.'

'Mr Stayner had never known any name but Art. Was that your husband's nickname?'

'Never. No one ever uses his middle name in any form.'

'He was always called Ralph?'

'I have always called him Ralph. A lot of his friends when we first met used to call him Raw, from his initials, but he didn't—'

'Raw. So they did know his middle name.'

'They knew his initials. I don't remember anyone knowing what the A stands for.'

'You were saying that your husband didn't—?'

'Was I? Oh! I was probably only going to say that he didn't really like being called Raw.'

'No. So he might ask people to call him Art instead.'

'He certainly would not. It's not the sort of name—' Some movement of Jack's caught my attention—or was it some extra quality in his silence? He was sitting as motionless as ever when I looked at him, but it pulled me round. 'It doesn't make any difference—does it?—what he might or might not be called, seeing the dead man is not my husband.'

'We have no proof of that.'

'Except my identification.'

'Exactly. Only yours.'

I was beginning to dislike the inspector.

'Did the Romford Street people tell you the colour of Art's eyes?' Jack's intervention was probably designed to cool the atmosphere rather than to acquire knowledge, but he had picked a subject the police might not have chosen to raise just then. The inspector answered not very happily.

'Mr Weatherley had gone about nearly all the time in dark glasses. There are lots of junkies do that. So the two witnesses weren't really agreed. But once they saw the corpse had brown eyes, that settled it for them. They were never in any doubt about it being their man. You were the only one, Mrs Weatherley—'

I interrupted him. 'Which of the two said Art had blue eyes?'

'I don't remember. They were neither of them very certain.'

The constable, hitherto silent, gave a little cough, and proudly produced his open notebook. 'It were Mayhew,' he said confidently, and read out: 'Stayner: You couldn't tell through those goggles whether he had eyes at all, but I got an idea they were brown. Mayhew: Wrong again, Tim. Sleeping in the same room, I often saw him awake before he had time to pull his glasses on and hide those baby blue eyes. Inspector: Perhaps if the curtains were drawn you couldn't—Mayhew: No curtains, Officer.' The constable's writing and reading of shorthand were impressive. I looked at him with new respect.

The inspector was growing impatient. 'Anyway, they made no bones about it once they saw the brown eyes there in the mortuary. Mr Mayhew withdrew handsomely and admitted he must have been mistaken. Perhaps you'd like to do the same now, Mrs Weatherley.'

'No. There is no doubt whatever that my client had blue

eyes. I wonder—' I hesitated. I do not like to do the police's work.

The inspector himself dropped the subject. 'At least we know now where he was living and who he thought he was.'

I let it go and saw them out. The others who had been waiting had given up and gone. No one else had come. I was not surprised; the rain was worse than ever. I decided we might as well have lunch early. It was a day to let old Sam stay by the gas fire to eat the rolls and over-ripe fruit he would have collected from the market gutters the evening before. I bolted the big outside swing door, locked behind us my office and the door into our passage and went into the kitchen with Jack.

## II

Over lunch I told Jack about our C.A.B.—it kept my mind off more personal problems. He has a quick mind and perhaps his sociology did help. He grasped quickly what I see as the various roles of any Citizens' Advice Bureau: to provide information, especially through the maze of welfare legislation and local services; to give positive advice where that is relevant and really asked for; and much more often, if one is competent to do so, to counsel, to listen and patiently enable one's client to find for himself what is the right way for him. I dwelt feelingly on the special needs of our neighbourhood:

'I know some C.A.B.s don't do any counselling, but here that's half the job. In an area like this, full of old people, with low earning capacity—the children if they do manage to get a good education can't find anywhere to live if they want to come back to the area—'

I think Jack murmured, 'There's always a ditch,' but I was in full flow and took no notice.

'And now of course there are the immigrants. There

always have been immigrants in Spitalfields, one wave after another. They add their special problems of language and different social customs and perhaps illegal entry and enormously worse housing problems. If you manage to suggest solutions, nice external, objective, attainable solutions, to a tenth of our clients' problems, you feel you've done miracles. After that all you can do is help build them up themselves, give them confidence again that they are real, nice people—'

'And that other people are real and nice too?'

'Yes. Yes, that comes next. But most of my people need confidence in themselves first.'

It was good to have a new mind on which to try out the job.

We went back through the waiting-room. With old Sam in there all through the lunch-hour, the scent of the flowers had not helped much. Before unbolting the outside door, I showed Jack the essentials of the office: the day-book in which every enquiry is meticulously entered —'and we analyse them at the end of the year and that gives support to the things we're pressuring our MP for'; the lists of hostels and helpful agencies in my top drawer; the directories and reference books on the shelf behind me. He was so quick a learner that I was tempted to try him on his own at once. But when I opened the big door, a man stood dripping on the doorstep, and I decided I should deal with him at least.

'Sorry. I should have opened earlier. I didn't know anyone had come in this weather. Why don't you leave your coat here? It will dry off a bit in front of the fire.'

I took him into my office and was glad to find Jack had discreetly settled himself at the little table, with an open book beside him and a sheet of paper on which he had already started writing—a splendid image of a man too busy to pay any attention to my affairs.

But this was not a local client—one of those from the City, perhaps. He had an inquisitive, foxy face. He looked at Jack's busy profile, turned back to me and said:

'I should like to speak in confidence, please, Mrs Weatherley.'

Jack pretended not to hear but I know an obstinate client when I see one so I said: 'I needn't keep you any more, Jack,' and he went.

The new client wasted no time.

'We've been hoping you could give us a little help, Mrs Weatherley,' he said, as soon as Jack had shut the door behind him. For a horrid moment I thought he was from the police, but he went on: 'I'm investigating on behalf of two or three insurance companies'—he probably was an ex-policeman—'all of them rather concerned about some of the recent fires round here. I'll name no names but more than one of the claimants have been extraordinarily lucky to be able to put in big claims just when they did.'

I remembered my naïve young client the day before. But her uncle was dead and could no longer be responsible. Oddly typical of our work that these two should come on successive days. Fortunately my client expected no comment at that stage and carried on with his carefully worded little speech.

'Now we understand that you know the people round here pretty well, good and bad. And that you're quite a hand at investigating a problem yourself, Mrs Weatherley. So we wondered if, with your ear to the ground, you sometimes get a whiff of something not quite right going on'—perhaps the metaphors were not very adequately prepared after all—'you'd just pass a word along to us. There's one or two little rumours blown our way already about a big place almost across the road from you. I'll name no names but you'll have a good idea what I'm talking about. There's some stuff going in and some say a lot of stuff coming out. But if it was to burn down to-morrow, my clients would almost certainly have to part with more thousands than it's healthy to think of.'

He was easy not to listen to and my mind wandered away to the big warehouse he spoke of. I'd heard the rumours too—of the truckloads of stuff being moved out, after the Lane had put away its stalls for the day—stuff that might still be listed in a fire insurance claim. I was wondering whether there was anything I could and should tell him, when the tone of his voice changed slightly, caught my attention again and destroyed my sympathy.

'It's extraordinary what people will do for money,' he said, rather unctuously. 'I think you'd be surprised. Some people would do anything. My companies must protect their policy-holders, and I can assure you, Mrs Weatherley, that if one of your cases dropped a few unguarded remarks that you could pass along to us to save our having to pay out, we'd know how to express our gratitude.'

'Some people would do anything for money,' I agreed. I got to my feet, and with Jack's 'I just don't want to be rich' echoing somewhere in the back of my mind, I added, 'And some would not. If I ever have any direct evidence of criminal intent, my clients probably expect me to give some warning to the police, but they certainly do not expect me to sell their "unguarded remarks" to anyone else.' Still standing, I turned to the day-book and said, 'May I have your name, please?'

But he too was angry now and perhaps, unexpectedly, a little scared—not able to recognize where he had gone wrong in his approach to me. He was unwilling to say any more.

I showed him out, collecting his still wet coat from the waiting-room, and found Jack standing there, gazing out at the rain.

'I'm sorry. Didn't Kevin tell you that your side-door key, that lets you into the part where we live, opens the communicating door from there into the C.A.B. too? We call it the double key, and you have to treasure it as irreplaceable. You could have used it to go through, and been doing something.'

'I've been thinking—much more useful.'

'And I've been losing my temper again. I really am

going downhill.'

'You suppress too many emotions. They have to come out somewhere.'

He might be right at that, but I wasn't going to tell him.

'Well, I didn't let this one come out much. But he tried to buy me—after telling me oilily that some people will do anything for money!'

Jack laughed. 'I wish I'd heard that emotion being allowed to come out just a little.'

My own laughter was not very spontaneous. I had too much on my mind. There were no more clients in the waiting-room and with the rain throwing itself down as it was, there might be no more that day. It was not yet three.

'Jack. Thinking might be good for me but there are things I want to do too. Could you bear to hold the fort for the next hour or two? There may be nobody else today, and if there is, I think you'll probably cope very well. There'll be phone calls, of course, but you can list any difficult ones for me to call back. If you're stuck, I'll be in the house. I'm not going out, so you can just come through and call me for anything you feel is really urgent. But I'll come in again before five. OK?'

'I take it as a compliment. But don't try to do everything yourself, Kate. There's Kevin and me about, remember.'

'I won't forget, thank you. But Ralph Arthur Weatherley —he sounds like my responsibility.'

I took the key of the office off my ring and gave it to him. The filing cabinet was already open and he would not need the safe—I never part with that key anyway. The outer door is fastened only with a bolt, and I checked that he did have a 'double key' for the connecting door. Then I went through it myself.

### III

I seemed to have been doing my thinking already—I was not sure when. I went to the phone in the passage and recovered the little piece of paper on which last night I had written Jill's phone number. It was tucked between two phone books. I went up the stairs with it to Agnes's big sitting-room on the first floor. She always urges me to use it when she goes away—after all, I am her deputy. To phone on her extension is more comfortable—and more private—than from the hall.

Jill answered when I rang her number. She had none of Rex's little tricks. She just said: 'Hullo! Hullo! Jill Metcalfe here.'

'Hi, Jill! This is Kate Weatherley. We all wanted to let you know how dreadfully sorry we are about Art. That's a terrible thing to happen in a close group like yours—and when you had all been trying to help him through. Tell the others how sorry we are, will you? We feel we know you all after last night.'

Jill made acknowledging noises the other end. She sounded pretty low. I carried on. I hate busybodies.

'Had he any family—people you can get in touch with?'

She sounded—thank goodness—quite glad to talk.

'It's awful. We can't find a soul. Most people seem to know him through us. And—you won't believe it—we find we don't even know his name. He told Rex and me some time—we don't either of us remember just when—he was rather funny about it and then never mentioned it again—that his name was Ralph Arthur Weatherley—the same surname as yours. But the police seem to think he might be making it up.' I was glad to hear it. It was more than they had admitted to me. 'Not that a name helps much at this stage.'

She sounded on the verge of tears.

'Jill, I don't know if the police told you that Ralph Arthur Weatherley is the name of my husband. Art

wasn't my husband, but it looks as though he was pretending to be. Naturally I want to know why. And if we
once found that out, we might even start finding out who
he really was and if there are people you ought to be
telling. Are you free now? I wondered if you could
possibly come over here. I can't come over to you, because I'm really in charge of the C.A.B., though Jack is
in there doing what he can for a bit.'

The idea of action had calmed her as I had hoped it
might. But reluctantly she explained that she could not
leave the house.

'I've promised Lorraine I'll let in a visitor of hers if he
arrives before she gets back. All the others are out, so I
think I must stay in. Can't I help on the phone?'

I would much rather have had her with me. Visible
reactions are often more revealing than words. I wondered
briefly if I could possibly leave Jack, but after my self-
righteous refusal ever to let anything interfere with the
running of the Bureau—only yesterday I had made the
police wait until two for me to go to the mortuary—I
could not possibly just walk out leaving it in totally
inexperienced hands the first moment my own interests
were involved. And for some reason I could not wait. I
had a wholly irrational feeling that the scent might run
cold. So the phone it had to be.

'Right-oh, Jill, if you don't mind. But it does seem to
concern me as well as you.'

She was accommodating and helpful and, as I had
noted already, only too glad to have someone to talk to
about Art. The only trouble was that she had so little to
tell.

Art had been with them about six months. She could
not remember who had introduced him. She thought
perhaps Tim had met him at a party and brought him
back with him. But she had asked Tim about it at lunch
that day and Tim could not remember if that was how it
was. Sheila had said that she had thought it was Rex
who had first met him but Rex could not remember that

either. Somehow or other Art had swum into their circle
six months before, stayed a night, as it seemed countless
visitors did, after or before parties or on their necessary
way through London, and had never gone again. He
sounded like a Londoner, but come to think of it, he had
never, so far as Jill could remember, brought in any other
friends. He had been co-operative and reasonably friendly,
but unreliable 'of course', as Jill said, from the depths of
her ageless experience of junkies. On occasional bad days
he had threatened suicide. They had made him a formal
member of the commune partly to bolster his self-respect
and help with his 'problems'. She could not think off-hand
of any special problems except the heroin. Oddly enough,
money was not a problem. He was a registered addict and
the clinic's supply would appear, most unusually, to have
made it unnecessary for him to be spending all his funds
on additional supplies. He had seemed flush with funds,
paid his weekly sub to the commune, been a bit extrava-
gant and experimental on clothes, and within the commune's scrupulous regard for individual autonomy, had
never found it necessary to tell anyone where those funds
came from.

Mentally I compared our own more conformist community and decided we came out unexpectedly badly in
the fields of autonomy and privacy.

'This call will cost you a fortune,' said Jill.

'I know. Let's hurry on. There's just the name and the
party.'

On the name there seemed nothing to add. He was
always known as Art. Tim and Sheila said they had heard
no other name.

The party was more interesting. They had been meaning for some weeks to run a party, but the previous week
Art had suddenly started urging them to have it at once.
He had wanted it at the weekend, and when it turned out
that Rex and Jill were both going to be away, had almost
insisted on Monday as the last possible day.

'Did he say why?'

'No. And being as he was, you couldn't really push him about things. Then when we'd agreed and started arranging it, he said we must ask you people from the Spitalfields Residential Settlement. He wouldn't say who or why, just that he wanted you all. He was really funny all last week, very edgy and difficult. He had said before, once or twice, something about having some connection down at the Settlement. He'd only sort of hinted at it, as if he was boasting a bit. That was why I'd thought of your C.A.B. as a place to come and ask about Lorraine. All I said about that really was true. It was only coming yesterday, in spite of being busy with the party, that was due to Art having pushed so much. And of course asking you to the party. That was for Art, though in the end we were awfully pleased you did come.'

'So are we. And what had happened with Art on Sunday? Which of you saw him last?'

But Jill had no chance to answer. Jack shouted up the stairs: 'Kate, the police are here to see you again.'

To my surprise, they came up the stairs and into the room even as he spoke.

I started to say down the phone, 'I'm sorry. I'll have to—' but one of the police took the receiver from my hand. He said:

'Who is that? . . . Miss Jill Metcalfe? In Romford Street. Right. We'll be in touch with you again.' He hung up.

It was the same inspector I had begun to dislike this morning, and his manners had deteriorated. I stood up, trying to find a really crushing remark, but Jack had followed the two police in and spoke first.

'I do apologize, Kate. I had no intention of letting these two gentlemen'—the emphasis was a little overdone— 'into this part of the house. Your phone was engaged so I was coming through myself to fetch you.'

Perhaps the police recognized, as I did, that this wordiness was an attempt to give me time to think. The inspector broke in sharply.

'It is Mrs Weatherley we have come to see.'

'She is not obliged to see you on her own. Would you like me to stay, Kate?'

I was feeling browbeaten by the unlikeable inspector, so I said: 'Yes, thank you, Jack. That would be kind.'

But suddenly, as he started, with his usual effortless competence, to move up chairs for the police and himself, I found myself wondering whether I was right to describe this stranger, Jack, as kind, or whether it was primarily a desire to hear what the police wanted that had brought him up hard on their heels. I stood, hesitating, while the two police sat down rather ill-temperedly, and Jack stood waiting for me to sit down again, looking at me. My uncertainties vanished with a sudden remembrance of the empty C.A.B. below.

'Oh! Of course not, Jack. I'd forgotten the C.A.B. We can't leave it empty. I expect to come down and take over anything outstanding about half past four.' I looked at my watch. It had gone half past three. Jill had been right about the expense of that phone call.

Jack gave me a little nod and went, unsmiling. I thought the inspector would look pleased, but the grim lines relaxed not at all. I sat down and waited for him to tell me what was the matter.

'We shall have to know more about your husband, Mrs Weatherley. Can you give us—'

'Why, Inspector?'

'Can you give us his present address?' He was pursuing his usual policy of ignoring my questions. I tried it too.

'I asked why, Inspector.'

He paused a moment, and then said tightly: 'New information received. May we please have your husband's present address?'

'May I know the new information? It apparently concerns my husband and myself.'

'I am not at liberty to divulge it at the moment. May I have your husband's address?'

'No.' He began to turn an explosive red and I added quickly: 'I don't know it.' If he was not going to tell me anything anyway, I might as well help him simmer down. 'I have not seen my husband for over six years. I have not heard from him for five. We used to exchange Christmas cards but the last I sent came back "address unknown".'

'But you know he's alive?'

'The solicitors would let me know if he died.'

'He might have changed his solicitor.'

'He may not even have a solicitor. It's the one that administers his grandfather's will that counts, Pendle, Son and Pendle, and he can't be changed.'

'And does that solicitor know where you are living?'

'Certainly. I've always told him of my moves.'

'So that you could be quite certain of not losing your inheritance.'

I looked at him in genuine surprise. 'I'm not the one to inherit. It was *Ralph's* grandfather's will.'

'We know all about that, Mrs Weatherley. And that you would be the one to inherit, if your husband died soon enough.'

'Would I? I don't think we ever discussed that. We were young, nine years ago. We never thought of either of us dying.'

'But you've thought about it a lot lately, haven't you, Mrs Weatherley? Only four more months to go before you lose the lot, isn't there? You've thought about those dates a lot, haven't you, Mrs Weatherley?'

What absurd nonsense was in his mind?

'What *is* all this about? I don't understand how any of this, anything to do with Grandfather Bloxham's will, concerns you.'

'You don't, Mrs Weatherley? You deny that you've been thinking about those dates, about next June coming up?'

'Of course I've been thinking about dates—when to start divorce proceedings.'

'Divorce! With all that money at stake. You don't

expect anyone to believe that, Mrs Weatherley?'

'Inspector, if you don't believe what I say, there is no point in continuing this conversation.' I stood up and found, to my annoyance, that I was shaking, but I went to the door and opened it. 'I am going down to the C.A.B. now. Can I show you out first?'

Rather to my surprise, they went, the inspector saying only, 'We'll be coming back.'

IV

I had difficulty keeping my mind on the C.A.B. that next hour. Jack had made full entries in the day-book—in a surprisingly small handwriting, like a doctor's. Those calls he could not cope with he had listed for me to ring back, and doing so took much of the time, with few interruptions —the rain was lessening, but it was too late in the day for enquirers to set out.

While I was on the phone to some remarkably long-winded man—Jack had been able to do nothing with his enquiry, which seemed at first to deal with the number of pet-shops in the area and whether there was a need for one, but which kept turning aside into enquiries as to the sex life of dogs, cats and other mammals—Jack went out to the kitchen. He came back with two welcome cups of tea—I had been trying to refresh myself with water— and the news that Kevin was already home. At Jack's suggestion—he showed an enthusiasm for learning which overcame my current lack of interest—we spent the last twenty minutes going over the cases he had dealt with, so that I could tell him anything he had omitted to do.

He smiled ruefully as we finished looking at the last case. 'That's only two, out of that whole lot, where I've done all that could be done. Not too good.'

'Nonsense. Every worker deals with cases a bit differently. But it would be sad if all my experience and training went for nothing and you knew as much as me on your first day. That enquiry about how to grow avocado pears, you dealt with splendidly—much better than I would have done.'

At exactly five we locked up, urging poor old Sam out into the rain first. He sleeps in a hostel where he's not allowed to spend the day. Ever since I've known him he's been too senile—I wonder if there's such a thing as life-long senility—for much communication, but these last few months he seems to have belonged less and less to the human family.

Kevin was not in the kitchen when we went through, but the fire was on and there was plenty of tea still in the teapot.

Jack said, almost at once, 'What's wrong, Kate?'

Sipping my hot tea and wondering how much to tell him, I had to give him full marks for professionalism: in the C.A.B. he had concentrated, and kept me concentrated, on the job. On the other hand a kinder person— it was always his kindness I found myself questioning— would surely have recognized my reluctance to talk, and helped me out. He added no more questions but he sat looking at me with those relentless brown eyes, waiting for my reply, in a silence that was itself a powerful form of pressure.

I might have succumbed to it if Kevin had not come back just then. He put two bags of mushrooms on the table and smiled at us both.

'J-just squeaked into that h-handy greengrocer in time. Wasn't that lucky? H-has Jack told you about our plans?'

'I hope you don't mind, Kate. Kevin has rung Jill and Co. and invited them round to supper. I'll help Kevin get it ready, of course. We're both passable cooks.'

I decided Jack must have a strongly stimulating effect on Kevin; he had never taken such an initiative before.

'That's a very good idea. Whatever made you think of it, Kevin?'

'I-it was Jack wh-who suggested it. H-he thought they'd all be h-horribly low and we could give them a bit of a break.' Whether once more Jack's motive was kindness or inquisitiveness, I decided then not to tell him about the police's renewed interest in me—and Ralph. 'It was Rex wh-who answered when I rang, and h-he seemed quite keen on the idea. H-he said the four of them would love to come. H-he didn't say anything about Lorraine.'

'They insist she's not one of them.' Before Jack had a chance to start questioning me again, I added quickly: 'When are they coming? Our usual six-thirty? Give me a shout if you need help. I'll go and lie low till then. I'm so glad you've arranged it, Kevin.'

I smiled at him, and had to include Jack in the smile when he opened the door for me. He was looking straight at me but did not smile back. A disturbing man, I thought, as I went slowly up the stairs. Or was it just my own disturbance that I was projecting on to him?

v

I did not stay long in my own room, just long enough to loosen my hair, brush it out and pin it loosely up again— one of the most relaxing activities I can indulge in when I have only a few moments to spare. And I felt I had only a few moments to spare, with my mind racing and my inexplicable sense of urgency growing. I changed into slippers and went down again to Agnes's room, to the phone.

I had no need to look up the number I wanted. Susan is a very old friend; we were at college together and now we are both in London, we rely on each other a good deal. She offers me a friendly, sympathetic, stable base, where I can, when I need, escape from the tensions and close-knit commitments of settlement life in Spitalfields. I am less certain what I offer her—perhaps a sense of community, or even the very tensions that her smooth life lacks. But today I was not looking for escape hatches.

'Sue? How are you? . . . I'll tell you one day . . . Yes,

you can, though I feel rather guilty at asking you when
you are so busy yourself . . . I know, I know. A destructive
luxury, guilt . . . Oh! But we transmute it in the end—
quite constructively, I sometimes think . . . Alas! It will
have to wait. I need your help, now, if not sooner . . . No.
I'm talking nonsense. It's tomorrow I really want you to
do something for me. Would you, with all your medical
contacts, know which are the hospitals or clinics issuing
heroin to registered addicts—our end of London, I guess,
not yours . . . Good . . . Good . . . But it's not as easy as all
that. What I need is some quiet but rapid enquiries as to
whether any of them were dealing with a thirty-five-or-
so-year-old man, tall, thin, with long, straight, fair hair,
if that's any help, who went by the name of Art, presumably Arthur. He might have given an address in
Romford Street, E.1, but he might not. Do you think
there's any chance at all? . . . Yes. Fortunately Arthurs
aren't found under every bush these days, and I think
I've got the age about right . . . No. I know it's difficult
to tell with junkies, but I don't think he was that far
gone . . . What I desperately want is the surname, and
anything else you can get, of course . . . Yes, of course.
You'll have the whole gloomy saga as soon as it's safely
wound to a conclusion . . . You're a tonic. I'll hope to hear
from you very soon . . . Yes. Yes, I am. You're wonderful.
'Bye, Sue.'

I looked at my watch. Time was moving too fast. I
dialled another number. While it was ringing, I could hear
Jack's voice—he has an unmistakable, deep voice—up-
lifted in song.

'Norman. Could you arrange to get some information
for me tomorrow?' Norman is not so old a friend, and he
is an exceedingly busy solicitor, but I made no apologies
this time. Requests for help are as welcome to suitors as
crusts to a starving man. I distribute them sparingly only
for my own self-respect. 'I need the details of a will . . .
Yes . . . Rather urgently . . . My husband, Ralph Arthur
Weatherley, had a maternal grandfather, name of Blox-

ham . . . No. Sorry. I think that's the only name I ever
knew. The old man died six years before we were married,
and that's ten years ago. That makes it . . . Yes. That must
be right. Just sixteen years ago . . . Yes . . . He left a pretty
complicated will . . . Yes. One of those that try to make sure
everybody does what the testator thinks is right for years
after he's dead . . . Yes. Ralph was the one who had got to
toe the line, and the conditions were quite detailed . . .
No. I never saw the will, just heard the details, or at least
some of them. Is that difficult? I'll be very grateful indeed.
. . . Yes. If I could have them tomorrow, that really
would be good . . . No. I know we haven't. When this
particular crisis is over, I'll come and tell you all about
it . . . How's sister Cynthia? . . . Yes . . . Yes . . . I can just
imagine it . . . *Pour passer le temps*, no doubt. Right,
Norman, I'll be hearing from you . . . Thank you . . .
Goodbye.'

The only other call I wanted to make needed office
hours, so it would have to wait till tomorrow.

I went out of the room and as I closed the door behind
me I heard the kitchen door below me close too. I waited
a moment for Kevin or Jack to come upstairs, but there
was no sound from the hall, only from the kitchen, where
I could hear voices now—but no song. So someone must
have gone into the kitchen, out of the hall, where the
other telephone extension is always available for anyone
to eavesdrop on phone conversations upstairs. 'And
where our coats hang, for anyone to go out of the kitchen
and pick up the pen or notebook or handkerchief they've
left in a pocket,' I said to myself fiercely, as I went up to
my room. 'Stop being so paranoid, Kate.'

## VI

Our Settlement's social entertainment is considered by
our friends to be one of our more acceptable activities.
Much of it is casual and unplanned, a happy acceptance

of uninvited droppers-in. On the rare occasions when we
do arrange a party, big or small, we have made a habit
of putting in the necessary work well in advance and are
then free to relax on the day. In my preoccupation, I not
only overlooked the effect on us all of recent death and
unsolved deception, but I overlooked too the absence of
many of our usual ingredients, especially of the group of
devoted, supportive Residents. I took it for granted that
the evening would be the usual success. It was not.

I must have been in the bathroom when the guests
came, running water drowning the sounds of their
arrival. So I went on brooding, and tidying myself and
my room without hurry, thinking they were late. When at
last I went down, late myself, they had been there more
than ten minutes. They were sitting stiffly on our straight
chairs, some distance from the electric fire, which is our
only source of heat—and for some reason the voltage was
down that evening, so both heat and light were comparatively feeble.

Jack, without explanation—he never did give an
explanation—had slipped out of the house just before
they arrived, and I had been loitering upstairs, so for ten
minutes Kevin was their only host. As it was he who had
phoned and invited them, they only too probably got the
impression that he was the only one who wanted them.
I am sure he must have welcomed them most warmly,
but the stammer, which does not appear to worry him,
is disconcerting to many of his listeners.

As I came in he was saying 'D-do come nearer this
h-horrid fire. Once you h-have got wet, and I expect you
h-have all got h-horribly wet, you really must make sure
you're h-hot.' From their reactions I concluded he had
said much the same several times already.

I feared apologies would add to the negative atmosphere, so I set out to be positive.

'It really is good to see you all here,' I began.

'We're not all here,' said Sheila.

There were indeed only three of them.

'We guessed Lorraine might not come, but I'm—'

'Lorraine isn't one of us,' Sheila insisted.

'I'm sorry Tim hasn't been able to come with you.'

My remark coincided unfortunately with a fresh effort by Kevin, who said at exactly the same time:

'H-how nice for Tim to h-have been invited to that do.'

'Very lucky for him.' Sheila's shyness had given way to something less helpful.

Rex decided it was time he came in. 'We're all of us a bit off key at the moment. Art going has really thrown us. Very heavy.'

Given this lead, Jill too pulled herself out of her unhappy, isolating thoughts. 'There's still a lot we want to talk to you about. I'm so glad you asked us over.'

'There's nothing we want to talk about, if you mean about Art.' I had not recognized Sheila's assertiveness the night before—perhaps I had been too busy admiring Jill's attractions. 'Art's dead. He was a weight on us all and the quicker we stop gassing and guessing and sentimentalizing about him, the better.'

The silence to which this reduced us was broken by the sound of Jack letting himself into the hall, and presumably hanging up his wet macintosh. He was singing as usual, quietly but clearly in his deep voice:

'Oh, I could be a conductor,
But then I might get in a wreck.
In any case a uniform
To me is a—'

He broke off as he came into the kitchen. 'Hullo. Have we all been in a wreck?' Not only does Jack not miss much, he does not mind commenting on what he sees, either. 'Come on, Kev, let's get that meal on the table quickly and see if our cooking is any good as a restorative. Kate has allowed Kevin and me to experiment on you people tonight.'

Rex went to help them, while Sheila said to me, 'Can I use the loo?'

I took her to the bottom of the stairs, pointed out the bathroom door on the half-landing and went back to talk to Jill. She was not trying to help the men—just sitting. She was very low still.

'You were a great help on the phone, thank you, Jill. After supper perhaps you can tell me about Sunday. That's where we were interrupted.'

'Yes. Was it the fuzz again, talking to me like that? Goodness! They can be so rude!'

'S-supper up.'

'Where's Sheila now?' Rex does go on at her, I thought, and then remembered it was Lorraine he had been attacking the previous night. His suave manners do not go very deep.

We had to wait for her so long, the meal cooling on the table, that I went to see if she needed something. But she met me as I opened the door. She made no apologies but looked at the table and said:

'Didn't Jill tell you—?'

She had reached the table by then and I think Jill kicked her, so we did not hear then what Jill might have told us. After this somewhat awkward beginning, the meal itself was the best part of the evening. I don't know how Kevin and Jack had divided their functions but between them they certainly can cook. The grill was varied, well cooked and well served, and the jam soufflé which followed—something I have never attempted— melted in our mouths exactly as intended.

Sheila made an obvious effort to overcome her bad temper—equivalent in her, I suppose, to Jill's low spirits— and congratulated the men warmly on their skill in the kitchen. Jill ate very little of the grill, and Kevin, who was clearly much taken by her, kept pressing her to have more, until she said, with a rather rueful version of her wide grin:

'I didn't mean to tell you, and I stopped Sheila telling you, that I'm usually a vegetarian. I'm not a fusser. I always try to eat whatever people have been working hard at preparing for me. But I seem to be losing my taste for meat. But you've lots of other protein here. Just don't worry about me.'

'I-if it's keeping off meat h-helps you to dance like that, it's h-high time we all—'

'Why?' asked Jack. 'Why are you a vegetarian?'

'It's one tiny, tiny contribution to sharing the world's food more fairly. Makes me feel less greedy anyway. We started as a vegetarian commune, macro-biotic and all that, but once Jim had gone, I seemed the only enthusiast left, badly outnumbered and outclassed once Rex joined us. He's a proper carnivore.' She flashed him a brief grin.

'Y-you don't look, Rex, as if you're oversupplied with meat.' Perhaps Kevin was a little envious of Rex's figure. He has to struggle to keep his own.

'We none of us overeat, meat or vegetables, except, of course, Lorraine.' Sheila had forgotten her refusal to count Lorraine as one of them.

'In a hungry world, overeating is rather obnoxious.'

'P-positively obscene!' Kevin hastened to support Jill.

'The most obscene thing in this field is that popular American operation where they take out part of a person's gut so she can go on guzzling as much rich food as she fancies and only absorb a small part of it.'

'Jack! You'll spoil our dinner!'

He smiled at me, without apology, and brought the conversation back to the commune. By mutual consent, we were waiting until after supper to talk about Art.

'What brought you all to this area?'

'Cheapest place to doss,' said Sheila, and added more unexpectedly, 'and there are some good people to doss with. I wouldn't have missed being with you, Jill.'

'It has been good, hasn't it?'

Rex enlarged: 'There are a lot of people like us round here, trying to find ways of getting out of the rat race, positively enjoying being downwardly mobile.'

'It's an interesting ambition. I wonder if this alternative life-style has spread here from the States. It takes a people very used to wealth to seek the virtues of poverty.'

'S-spoken like a sociologist, Jack.'

'Like an over-rich hobo, keeping well out of the ditch.'

By unhappy association, Jack's disclaimer brought us back to poor, dead Art.

## VII

Supper was over, but with no space for comfortable chairs in this, our only common room, we stayed where we were round the table, drinking Nescafé, only Kevin or I going out into the cold hall, whenever the phone interrupted us. I thought of inviting everyone up to my room, but, apart from the fact that it had had no fire on for the last hour, I was reluctant to break the improved atmosphere. So we sat on.

I turned to Rex, a young man of authority. 'Did Jill tell you that I feel involved with Art, seeing he was claiming my husband's name? I'm still hoping one of you can tell me who he really was and where he came from. But from what Jill tells me, none of you knows much.'

'Too right. We were all so busy trying to make him feel wanted and one of the group that we seem to have succeeded in rubbing out any other life he'd ever had. We can't think of any friends, except the ones we all have in common, nor any other addresses, and Tim and I differ on who first brought him along.'

'You think it was Tim?'

'And he thinks it was me. But then I was wrong about the eyes, so perhaps I'm wrong on this too.'

Jack and Kevin kept silent, leaving to me the invidious task of inquisitor, so I went on.

'What happened on Sunday—to Art, I mean? Was he depressed? Was he high? Had anyone any idea he was coming along here?'

Sheila, dropping back into her black mood, said: 'For God's sake! The guy's dead, isn't he? *And* he did it himself so no one else comes into it. Can't we let the bloody thing alone?'

'But he may have some family we ought to be in touch with.'

Rex ignored them both. 'We've been trying to decide which of us saw him last. It's more complicated than you'd expect. Jill, Sheila, Lorraine, Tim and me, we all went off to the Lane that morning.' This is the local term for Petticoat Lane market, with its stalls stretching down Wentworth Street, past our big C.A.B. door. 'We know it's dearer on Sundays, when all the tourists crowd in, but it's the only day we can all get down, and we enjoy watching the con tricksters.'

'Did Art go with you?'

'No. He wasn't usually up in time.'

'But funnily enough'—supper had revived Jill—'he was up quite early last Sunday. He'd put a coat over his pyjamas and was messing about in the kitchen, when the rest of us left.'

'You left together? Did you all stick together?'

'Heavens, no! We generally walk together as far as the Princess Alice, but after that we go in pairs, or the odd three if necessary. On Sunday, we didn't need a three after all. It was odd, so unlike Lorraine.'

Rex took over firmly. 'On Sunday, we didn't even all reach the Princess Alice. Just outside Toynbee, Lorraine said she thought she'd split as she'd got some things she wanted to do on her own. And she went across Commercial Street and under Denning Point, and that was the last we saw of her. When we turned into Wentworth Street, Jill and Sheila stopped to look at shoes, so I said to them, "Same time, same place," and went on with Tim. There was a real clown that we often listen to, auctioning—'

Jill interrupted this time, to explain a little belatedly, 'That means we'd meet as usual on the same corner, the Princess Alice corner, at one, and decide what to do for lunch.'

Rex abandoned the comic auctioneer. 'Tim and I got separated almost at once. I just mooched about. There wasn't anything I particularly wanted to buy. Then at one, the four of us met up as arranged.'

For once, neither Rex nor Jill seemed interested in going on. The lengthening silence seemed to have more significance than words so I said nothing, waiting to see which of the three would first find speech necessary. I had forgotten that Kevin can't stand silence.

'And wh-what did you do for lunch? H-have it out?'

'No. We went straight home.'

'We had lots of vegetables in the house that I thought we ought to eat up.' Jill's maternal housewifeliness always surprises me.

Rex wasted no time on such irrelevancies. 'When we got home, somewhere before half past one I should think, Lorraine was there. Art wasn't. She said she didn't know when he'd gone out. She knew he was still there when she got in, though she hadn't seen or talked to him.'

He stopped and the curiously awkward silence began again. Sheila broke it this time. 'Don't be so damned squeamish, Rex. The police know all about how one of you must be telling lies, so why shouldn't the do-gooders too?'

'Sheila, there might be some other explanation.'

'Oh yeah? I thought you were the one that claimed to be a realist, Jill, and now you go round hunting for imaginary strangers rather than admit that either Lorraine or your man or my man is lying in their teeth.'

'Rex isn't "my man".'

The kind Kevin and the civilized Rex both thought this the moment to break in. 'I-isn't it time for a drink? We are bad h-hosts.' But Jack caught his arm to silence him and left the floor to Rex.

'We're not helping you much, I'm afraid. As Sheila says, we've been over all this with the police, but you are welcome to hear it too. The trouble is we haven't found a reasonable explanation of it yet, unless Lorraine's hearing is as fallible as my eyesight has proved to be.' His mistake as to the colour of Art's eyes still rankled. 'She insists that when she went in, and we don't think she actually did much shopping but went almost straight home, she went first to the bog, and while she was there, she heard some-one come in, using the key, not knocking, and start slanging Art. When she came out into the main room, they were in my room—well, it was Art's room too. Poor old Art—'

'She says she thought it was Tim,' Jill interrupted.

'She thought it was Tim while she was still in the loo, but Tim stammering out abuse at the top of his voice, and he doesn't usually shout, so she doesn't claim to be sure. Once she came out into the main room, they must have heard her and dropped their voices, so she couldn't hear any words. She went into the kitchen to put some stuff she'd bought into the fridge, and when she came out they'd both gone. Tim says it wasn't him and I say it wasn't me, so you can take your choice.'

'C-couldn't it h-have been—' but Kevin was not being allowed much say that evening. Jack overrode him: 'What words did she hear of the shouting?'

Rex shrugged. 'Nothing much.'

'She says that Tim, or whoever it was'—Jill was not going to let us forget the probability that it had been Tim —'was telling Art off for a blundering fool, and if he didn't do better on Monday—'

'Well? If he didn't do better on Monday?'

'That seems to have been when the shouter heard Lorraine coming out of the bathroom and dropped his voice. So she never heard what the threat was.'

A knock on the outer door silenced us again. It was Jeff, the one who runs the food co-op. It seemed that Kevin, at the squatters' party, had urged him to look us up some evening, and he had wasted no time. He had two pleasant young men with him, from some Bethnal Green commune. We had to stop talking about Art, but at least the party livened up at last. They could only stay an hour, but everyone made good use of it, the talk, lively and cheerful, being mostly in two or three groups. I had been right about Jill's sex appeal, and I caught the tail end of one of Kevin's livelier tales of disaster: 'She's convinced now that I'm my brother.'

The newcomers had already had supper, but we drank vast quantities of coffee. Towards the end of their hour, the conversation became more political. Only the two strangers were hard-line Marxists but they had plenty to say for themselves. I had heard it all too many times and found my thoughts drifting back to our own problems, instead of listening, as I filled everyone's cup for the third or fourth time. I was jerked back to attention by a sudden silence, after some remark of Jack's, I thought. The whole table was listening, and he went on, after a pause:

'But your brand of communism is surely, to coin a phrase, so bourgeois, so depressingly bourgeois.' They were for once reduced to speechlessness and he went on: 'This conviction that everyone is motivated solely by economic interests, this passionate concern for the exact balancing of material gain; what could be more typical of a little French shopkeeper, the original bourgeoisie? Can't you find something more radical to work for?'

One of them managed to say, 'Like what?'

'You've plenty of choice. Have you ever tried giving people, especially the ones you think are trying to do you down, *more* than they expect or ask for? Or refusing to treat anyone as an enemy? Turning him into a friend takes a much more radical approach than fighting him. Or—' he looked at the pile of new records they had with them—'turning your back on wealth and seeing how simply you can live.'

'Oh! Religion,' said one, with sudden recognition.

'The opium of the masses,' added the other quickly, happy to find himself once more on the firm ground of his clichés.

Jack laughed out loud. 'Perhaps you don't know a real revolution when you see one.'

There were plenty of others ready to come in on that discussion, but the three had no more time to give us.

Jeff hung back to thank us. 'Sorry we can't stay longer. They're a really cool couple of guys till they start reciting the Word. I'll come back another evening, if I may.'

We came back into the kitchen to find Sheila already on her feet. 'Has your crowd got all you want about Art? If so, it's time we were getting back to dear Lorraine to see what fresh fantasies she's dreamt up to keep us all excited.'

'You think she invented the whole Sunday incident?' Jack got her reference quicker than I did.

'Obviously. She always has to be the centre of attention, as you may have noticed.'

Rex said, 'If one of us has to be lying, I'd put my bets on Lorraine. She doesn't know there's any difference between truth and lies. But then I'm prejudiced. What do you think, Jill?'

'It's funny, but I found her almost convincing for once. Isn't that stupid?'

'Yes,' said Sheila. 'Let's get home.'

She must have realized at once how ungracious this sounded, and, to do her justice, she tried to recover the situation. She said: 'Could you show us your C.A.B. before we go? Jill was telling me what a lovely big room you use as a waiting-room.'

So we all went across the hall into the waiting-room. It is an unusual room, stretching across the front of the house, with the big window that was installed in the days when it was used as a shop. It looked tidy and even pretty, with the flowers and without Sam.

'We use it for all sorts of other things. Tuesday, Tom usually has a group here practising, but he must have arranged something else for them tonight. Perhaps they've got a fixture somewhere—they do get asked to play, though we tell Tom *we'd* rather pay for them to keep away.'

'Th-they h-have improved these last few weeks. Didn't you h-hear them last Tuesday, Kate?'

'Who else uses the room? If we ever want to run a public meeting, could we hire it?'

'Sure, Rex.'

'And do you vet what it's wanted for? Would it have to be something you supported?'

'No. But it mustn't be something we're strongly opposed to either, like the National Front. That's our decision so far, though we're still arguing on whether, in spite of everything, we ought to give even them freedom of speech.'

'But they themselves don't believe in freedom of speech.' Jill was happy to join in our old argument and Jack came in too, but Sheila was uninterested in such fine points and stood fidgeting by the window. So I ended the discussion as soon as I could and took the party into my office to show them the books and pamphlets that are the tools of the trade.

Sheila did not bother to come in with us. She made it so clear that she was once more ready to go home, that they all rejected our offers of a final drink, thanked us, managed to say they had enjoyed the evening, and went out into the rain.

Their poor spirits had infected us. It was later than we had expected, so we agreed to leave the washing-up for Maggie, who comes on Wednesdays and Fridays now. As we were clearing the table, I said to Jack:

'So you really do mean that you don't want to be rich.'

'I look like it, don't I?'

I looked at him. He had changed for the evening into a particularly eye-catching shirt. He looked pretty good. He was looking at me too, but I turned away, without saying anything. I did not find him easy to understand.

He was at my heels as I went upstairs. When I reached my door he said, 'You're tough, Kate, the way you keep up.' It made me suddenly feel totally exhausted, ready to give in and cry on anyone's shoulder. It was as well he added, 'Good night. Sleep well,' and went on up the next flight to his room.

## VIII

There must be a broken bit of guttering we have never noticed. Lying in bed, I could distinguish the heavy drip on my window-sill even through the drumming rain, and the gurgling of the water as it reached the drains. Keeping my thoughts carefully on such immediate matters, I wondered whether I ought to ring our builder in the morning, or leave it for Agnes. She would be back on Saturday. Only three days in between. But broken guttering can be nasty. It can break away and fall on the head of someone below and then there would be another body in the gutter.

It was no use. My thoughts could find byways back to death and disaster, however hard I tried to steer them away. I might as well stop steering. I rolled on to my back and gave my thoughts free rein.

I thought of Art, dead, in spite of all his own and the little commune's attempts to rescue him from the quicksand of heroin addiction. And I thought, with continuing uncertainty, for I still could not distinguish him from Art, of the blue-eyed impostor, who had come to the C.A.B. But mostly I thought of Ralph, as he was when we got married, ten years ago.

I could hear my mother saying, 'Lots of people have and will love you, Kate, but thank God you've found someone to love.' And at first I had been surprised, because I liked to think of myself as a loving person. But of course, this love had been different, utterly different, and whatever had happened to that particular relationship, at least I knew for always what loving was. It had illuminated the whole world, the earth and the heavens, and its brightness had spread to everyone I met—even though, when Ralph had been about there was so little time for anyone else. 'The dust and stones of the street were as precious as gold . . . And young men glittering and sparkling angels . . . All things were spotless and pure and glorious; yea, and infinitely mine and joyful and precious.' Good old Traherne, he must have been born knowing love, being in love.

My thoughts would not stay in the light. They moved inexorably into the darkness of the following year, and I did not want to go that way. So I switched on the bedside lamp, fetched myself a glass of water from the corner basin, climbed back into bed and concentrated on trying to disentangle the problems of the last two days.

I put aside for the time the inexplicable existence of the client, distinguishable from Art only by his eyes. From my inveterate reading of crime novels, a possible solution to that problem glimmered on the horizon.

But how could I explain Art's claim to be Ralph? And why had the claim been made only to Rex and Jill, and perhaps to me through the client? And from which of our old friends had the client—I could not wholly ignore him, after all—known that Ralph, only Ralph in the whole world, had called me Kit? There had been dozens of friends in those halcyon days. I could not think where to begin on that question.

And what was Art's relationship with Lorraine? Why did they never speak? Where did she fit in? Or was Lorraine no part of the puzzle, just one of those individuals so wholly concerned with themselves that they can fit nowhere, but stick out uncomfortably in every situation?

What had driven Art to take a fatal overdose? Was it the threats and abuse of the unknown caller on Sunday afternoon? And what were those threats? And who was the caller? I spent a little time on that question. Tim, I hardly knew, but I felt I knew Jill, and she seemed happy with him. Rex? I would not put much past that competent young man—whatever Jill's views. And then there had been that somewhat curious reference to the caller stammering out his abuse. The immediate circle included only one stammerer. Why had we not pressed for more information on that point? I would have expected Jack to, even with Kevin there.

Jack. Why on earth should I see Jack as a problem? He was a stranger, and in this fog, any stranger was a potential problem. Kevin had known him all their lives, but then Kevin was not much more than a stranger. What else? Jack had a persistent curiosity and I had no means of knowing whether this was natural to him or was peculiar to this situation. And had anyone listened in from the hall to my telephone conversations?

I would be glad of the answer to those calls. And first thing tomorrow—no, today; it was already past midnight —I must make the third call I had planned, a call to old Grandfather Bloxham's solicitors. I hoped they would give me Ralph's address, but in any case they could confirm that he was alive and that would settle the police.

The police themselves had become my most urgent problem. Their first calls, on Monday and Tuesday mornings, had been in line with what I would expect. I did not much like the particular inspector who was handling the affair—I had not even bothered to discover his name—but they had dealt reasonably with a situation that had proved more awkward than they had anticipated. But on their visit this last afternoon, they had suddenly shown themselves hostile. I did not know why. Had they really said and meant 'information received'? Who could be giving them information, twisted, misleading information about me and my marriage? Art had given false information about his name, my husband's name, but he was dead. Who was now giving information to the police, trying to influence them against me? Someone who knew me. Someone I knew? It was this new situation that gave urgency to my sense that I had better find the solutions myself, and quickly.

I lay for a time, trying to think out a plan of action, but nothing looked practicable until the answers to my telephone calls came in. I was glad I had put two of them in that afternoon. I wished our dinner-party had gone better. I did like Jill. I would like to have heard her— Rex and Sheila too—on Art. I would like to have talked to Tim. I realized I was falling asleep, so I switched off the lamp and turned over on to my front, hoping that in my sleep my subconscious would work on the major problems.

I did not dream of Art or the client impostor, nor of Jill or Sheila or Lorraine. My dreams were all of Ralph and they were horrible dreams, in which time and again he was handing me over to the police for having murdered him.

# WEDNESDAY, 16 FEBRUARY

## I

WEDNESDAY MORNING was sunny and even warming up a little, quite unlike my mood. Absurdly, this made it worse, like having a heavy cold in midsummer. I had slept very badly most of the night, turning and tossing as I struggled to escape what, even in my sleep, I sometimes knew to be a dream. But although the place changed and the time changed and the police changed, the core of the dream itself, with all its undertones of horror, recurred persistently. As the first light glinted faintly behind my curtains, I fell at last into a deep and, as far as I knew, dreamless sleep, so deep that I was undisturbed by even the stall-holders' lively morning greetings.

When at last I woke and hurried downstairs, Kevin had already left for work. Jack greeted me.

"Morning, Kate. I hope that sleep's done you good.'

He looked at me pretty searchingly and refrained from saying that I looked as though I could do with more. 'Don't rush it. It's just on nine, so I've opened the C.A.B. door. There are one or two waiting already, so if you'd like, I'll take your office key and go in and get started. I can always get them to wait, if they're too difficult for my 'prentice hand. But at least it will start things moving, while you get a proper breakfast.'

'That would be terrific, thank you. I don't feel as if I'd be much use without breakfast this morning.'

I gave him the key off my ring, but when he had gone through into the C.A.B., I carried my cup of tea into the hall and phoned Pendle, Son, and Pendle. I was already through to the office and was waiting for them to fetch old Mr Pendle, when I heard a key in the front door and regretted not having gone up to Agnes's room once more.

But it was my good friend Maggie, our treasured 'help'. She nodded at me, smiling, and I waved at her as she went into the kitchen. She never eavesdrops, and anything not meant for her which she overhears accidentally, she seems to push from her mind at once—not from any lack of interest, but from a highly developed respect for human dignity. And this, in spite of my knowing much about her, and her work-shy husband, and her little defective daughter, Cheryl.

Mr Pendle came on the line with enquiries as to my health. We had known each other for ten years.

'I'm very well, thank you, Mr Pendle. And you? . . . And Mrs Pendle? . . . Ah well, the spring will soon be here, won't it? It's much warmer today, don't you think?' Is it the age of the other party or the relationship that reduces me to talking about the weather? 'I am needing your help, Mr Pendle. It is some years now since I heard from my husband and I don't think the address I have is the current one. I need to get in touch with him pretty urgently. Could you let me have his address? Or of course, if you'd rather, I could send him a letter through you, but that would delay me badly . . . Really? . . . I am surprised. He always used to let you know where he was . . . Changed the bank too! Then what do you do about the monthly money? . . . Yes. I understand. He rings you each month and tells you where to send it . . . a money order . . . I agree. It sounds very strange . . . How long has this been going on? . . . And when did he last phone? . . . Anyway, you'll be through with it all in June . . . Yes. Very near now . . . Thank you, Mr Pendle . . . Well, yes. Perhaps when he does phone next, you would just tell him I'm wanting to get in touch with him—very briefly. You've got this address, haven't you? . . . Yes, Wentworth Street . . . Yes. That's still the phone number . . . And you have the C.A.B. one too? . . . That's where you'll usually find me during the day . . . My regards to Mrs Pendle, please . . . Goodbye.'

Carrying my cup, I went slowly back into the kitchen.

I had even forgotten Maggie was there. She was making me some fresh toast.

'Come and have your breakfast quick, Kate. Whatever are you doing with the C.A.B.?' Maggie recognizes my priorities.

'It's all right. We've a new temporary Resident, Jack Winters, and he's—'

'Cousin of Kevin's. I remember.'

'Actually he turns out to be not quite a cousin. But he's —he's someone, all right, and he's helping out in the C.A.B. I overslept!'

'You look as if you could do with it. You're overdoing it. I shall be glad when the real Residents get back.' I wonder how long it takes to qualify with Maggie as a real Resident. But I shared her feelings. I should be glad too. 'Eat up now. Don't just play with it.'

'Well, you leave that sink and come and have a cup of tea with me. How's Cheryl?'

It was a relief to sit and relax with so old a friend. I found I was even tempted to talk about Ralph, as I had never done to anyone in the Settlement—only to Agnes, before she accepted me into residence. Now I had a hungry need to talk. But at this stage I could offer only problems, and goodness knows, Maggie has enough of those, for all her serenity. She knew already, of course, about the dead man in our gutter two days before—knew far more than we did. According to our neighbours, he had been a Russian spy—those who lifted him up to our door had recognized the bulge of a grenade in his pocket.

Maggie sniffed contemptuously. 'Too many people have too little in their minds. Leaves room for rubbish.'

I was glad to find I need not keep the news of Wendy Donovan's winning pool confidential; it was the talk of Spitalfields, with a good deal of sympathy for her un-conforming point of view, mixed with the inevitable envy.

'And it's not surprising in a district like this, Kate, that every Tom, Dick and Harry, the men more than the women, think they could make better use of the money than what the Donovans will.'

'I guess it's not many districts where people wouldn't feel that.'

I went reluctantly to the C.A.B. I wanted time to think, but that is a luxury we can rarely afford in the Western world as we have made it—unless we are overtired and lie awake at night, I reminded myself. And that makes for bad dreams.

II

However hard Jack had been working, the waiting-room was still full of people. A number were Asians—the big Bangladeshi community round us fits readily into the local rag trade—but a group of our nearer neighbours was standing near the door, gathered round Wendy Donovan. She broke away and came over to me. She was looking strained, somehow less sure of herself than in her dramatic tears yesterday.

'I know I oughtn't to see you out of turn, Mrs Weatherley, but it's not that I'm wanting any help. I just wanted to tell you, seeing you was the first to know yesterday, that there's nothing to come after all. Sean hadn't the money on hand for the postal order, so he never posted it.'

'Goodness, Mrs Donovan! What a shock for you! How's Sean taking it?'

'He's so mad with himself that he's taking it out on all of us. Real bad he is.' She raised her chin. 'But I'm going to tell him I'm glad—soon as I get a chance. The kids are just lying low till him and me have sorted it out.'

'But they're disappointed.'

'They've all had a bit of a cry. And now he says I've got to keep on harder than ever at the pools, do more than one a week. He reckons if I can get it right once, I ought—'

Jack had opened the office door to show a client out and it seemed that Wendy, with today's anticlimax, was not anxious to meet yet another of yesterday's admirers. She said, "Bye, Mrs Weatherley,' and slipped out with her band of supporters. I would tell Jack the story when all these would-be clients had gone.

I went through with him into the office.

'Anything urgent I ought to do before we go on?'

'No. I think I'm all right. But I'm glad you're back. I'm no expert on Asians.'

Jack slipped his papers from my desk to his own little one in the corner, as I opened the door to call in the next client. He came in humbly, hat in hand, with an unexpected resemblance to a suppressed Victorian servant, and was with difficulty persuaded to sit down. But he defeated me; the flood of words, when at last it came, recounting his urgent problem, included no word of English. With a sigh, I went back to the waiting-room, and from the Asian men still waiting there chose the best dressed, sitting a little by himself, and having checked that he spoke Bengali, invited him in to interpret.

Jack brought in another chair. The flood of words was repeated and when at last it slowed and stopped, I said:

'Now, I'll be most grateful if you will tell me his problem.'

The newcomer waved a dismissive hand. 'This is a man of no worth,' he said loftily. 'He is not one for you to trouble yourself with.' He turned to the first man: 'Go. Go back to where you have come from and do not trouble—' He did not choose to sink to using their mutual language but his tone and gestures were so unmistakable that the other man was rising and turning to go before I managed to break in and change the direction of the conversation.

My homily on the indestructible value of every human being would probably have been better, and certainly less self-conscious, if I had not been so aware of Jack, listening from his corner. But it was effective enough for the second man finally to accede, reluctantly, to my renewed request for interpretation. He even translated back to the client

—I hope, at least, that that was what he was doing—my advice on when and where to find Toynbee Hall's 'Poor Man's Lawyer', for it was legal advice he needed.

Then he surprised me by offering to go to Toynbee Hall with the client, to act as interpreter. But I realized just in time that he was expecting to be paid for this service, and I assured him that Toynbee's volunteer lawyers would have their own voluntary interpreter. They must do by now; today even the local banks have full-time interpreters, fluent in four or five Asian languages.

Showing the first man out, I offered to take the second out of turn, as some acknowledgement of his help. But he had lost all confidence in me; someone who insisted on spending so much time—and so much of his own precious time too—on the affairs of a valueless man was not the adviser he sought. So he went too, and as the others had apparently only been there to give the first man confidence and had gone with him, the waiting-room was now empty, but for the ever-present Sam.

I turned back into the office where Jack wanted to discuss the implications of the last case.

'How is it that Pakistanis and Bangladeshis and Arabs too, which means most Muslims, see anybody poorer than themselves as non-human? Is there anything in the Koran to encourage this?'

I started to say, 'Women, as well as the poor,' but he went on:

'Or is it just that there's nothing to discourage it? Is human nature basically nasty unless redeemed by a compassionate religion, and you can't—'

I went back to his first questions, not ready for a discussion on original sin.

'Jack, not all Muslims are like that. Some of the ones I know here are very helping, gentle people. The Koran insists on generosity to beggars—'

'And inhuman punishments to transgressors, cutting off hands, stoning—'

'You can't pick on just Muslims. Wait till you meet our

Jerry Steel, founder of the Spitalfields Self-Help Association. He covers up his less reputable views of course, wouldn't hurt a fly, so he implies, but there's no doubt of his basic philosophy: "Pull the ladder up, Jack; I'm all right." '

I looked out of the door again, but there was still no one waiting so I said, 'Let's go and have some coffee while there's no one here. We probably won't have another chance this morning.'

'And you can tell me about the Self-Help Association. It sounds a good idea in itself.'

'That's what we originally thought, voluntary, democratic, free of patronage by outsiders like us. And it's only slowly come home to us that these, the ones that have made it, are so busy consolidating their own position, making things better for their children—you can't blame them—that they don't want to know about anybody else, anybody with problems. Keep out the immigrants, prosecute the prostitutes, send the homeless somewhere else. It turns out that outsiders like us really do have our uses, and not just because of our better education, as the founding fathers of the Settlement thought, and not even because of our specialized training—'

'Just because of your objectivity, having no axe to grind,' said Jack. 'Alas for self-help! But can't the immigrants, and the prostitutes and the hobos, make their own self-help associations? Does it have to be only the more privileged?'

We had made the coffee by then and I shouted upstairs for Maggie, introduced Jack to her, and remembered that I must tell them both about Wendy's change of fortune.

'When she told you, what did you say to her?' asked Jack. 'It's like that old story of the man whose friend said, "Didn't you know, my wife's gone to heaven." ' He looked at us enquiringly, but as neither of us admitted to having heard the story before, he went on: 'And first he said, "I'm so sorry," and then he said, "I mean, I'm so glad," and then he said, "I mean, I'm so surprised." Which did you say?'

'I didn't say, "I'm so surprised." I'm not at all surprised. I bet Sean Donovan hasn't posted off any postal orders for months. I admit I never thought of that yesterday.'

When we went back to the C.A.B., I was annoyed to find that between us we had omitted to lock the office door. I am not used to being busy discussing original sin with a fellow worker. I took the key back from Jack and put it on my ring; I must keep a grasp of my responsibilities. There were two clients waiting. We had been lucky to have the Bureau empty for those few minutes, on a fine day after a wet one. It was never empty again the rest of the morning, however quickly I tried to handle each case. Jack dealt with some phone calls, while I was talking to clients, so that helped. But thinking about my own problems, my own case, was totally impracticable, until Jack, who was seeing clients out for me and bringing new ones in, most unexpectedly brought in Tim Stayner.

### III

Tim said, 'Hullo. Once you've met us, you can't get rid of us, can you? I'm working in that warehouse down the road. And do they keep you busy! But it's good money, and Sheila and I are saving to get across to Greece for a few months' holiday. As I was passing your Citizens' Advice Bureau, I thought I might as well just drop in. There are one or two things we wanted to mention to you.'

He was as thin and tall as ever but perhaps less confident, even with that hearty voice, than when I had met him in his own environment on Monday. He went on:

'I was sorry not to come round with the others last night. Sheila said you gave them a slap-up meal.'

'Jack and Kevin's cooking—nothing to do with me. All

I contributed was a lot of questions about Art—not a good way to make a cheerful evening, but he's a bit on my mind.'

'You bet. That's one of the things I thought I'd mention. There's going to be an inquest next Monday, and if no relatives have been found by then, the police suggest a funeral soon after that. We wondered if you felt involved.'

I shelved that for the moment and said, 'When did the police tell you?'

'This morning. They haven't told you?'

I shook my head. 'Thank you for letting us know. We'd be grateful if you'll give us a ring when the funeral is fixed.'

'Right. Only we're not really sure who's going to fix it. But I expect the police will be getting in touch.' I was sure the police would be getting in touch, but it did not seem necessary to say so. Tim went on, 'The other thing's Lorraine. She's getting on all our nerves rather badly at the moment, and we wondered—Jill's following up all your suggestions and we expect something will come of them, but we wondered if just for the moment she could possibly move in with you, to get her out of our hair.'

I was completely taken aback. We are, as Residents in an outreaching Settlement, heavily involved in the neighbourhood and its innumerable problems. At a pinch, we have slept homeless newcomers for one night on mattresses in the waiting-room—sometimes with unfortunate sequels. But the residential part of the house is our sanctuary, where we recover our breath in privacy among our carefully chosen fellows.

I looked across at Jack for support, and he clearly welcomed the opportunity to be drawn into the conversation, but what he said was: 'Wouldn't that be rather a good idea, Kate?'

I should like to have taken him aside and, firmly and rather coldly, explained to him how our Settlement functions, but this was not the moment, so I turned back to Tim and said: 'The other Residents will start coming back on Saturday, and it's already Wednesday. That wouldn't be much use to Lorraine.'

But Jack persisted. What's the good of his having penetrating eyes if he can't take a hint as broad as that? He said, quite out of turn, 'I gather Eric and Pam aren't expected back from Canada for some time. I'm using their bedroom, but wouldn't it be possible to make use of their sitting-room?' As our only resident couple, Pam and Eric share with Agnes the privilege of having a sitting-room of their own, as well as a bedroom.

'That would be absolutely marvellous. If we could get her away for just a week it would give us all a chance. We'd guarantee to move her again then, even if we had to take her back. I'll go and put it to her. Thanks a lot.'

He went—to put it to Lorraine—and I let him go. Talk about keeping a grasp of my responsibilities! I had not time to turn on Jack before he spoke. He only pretends to be dumb.

'Sorry, Kate. I hadn't realized you were so attached to your private ditch.'

'I told you—I don't like ditches.'

'I remember, and I've taken in that you'd like Lorraine here even less. But, Kate, if we're to find out what's going on, we must keep close to these people.'

'Why should they know any more than us?'

'Art was in it, whatever it is. And Lorraine seems to have had something on Art. Interesting that the rest of them should be prepared to push her out on to us.'

'They may also have their reasons for wanting to keep contacts with us.'

'They may indeed. I'd like to find out which of them started this particular push.'

'You're the most inquisitive person I know.'

'About some things. This touches you, Kate. Don't you want to find out what it's about?'

'It's too near. It's brought up memories that are making me a bit numb.' But I had no wish to talk about those memories, so I switched quickly. 'Tim's not a typical communard, is he? It's middle-class tourists who go to Greece.'

'And classicists. But you're right. The communards I know go to Nepal, or at least Morocco.' But his mind was on more practical matters. 'That funeral's coming up a bit fast. We can't leave the question of brown or blue eyes unsolved much longer.'

'You've the same idea as me then? You must read the same detective stories. *You* suggest it to the police. I'm on rather bad terms with them just now.'

I gave him their number and he rang through and asked for Inspector Brownfield—unlike me, he had troubled to find out his name.

'Inspector Brownfield? This is Jack Winters, from Spitalfields Residential Settlement . . . Yes . . . We've been thinking about the eyes of the man who died. We've been wondering whether the surgeon at the post-mortem found it necessary to examine the eyes carefully . . . Yes . . . We realize that . . . Yes . . . Yes . . . No. Our suggestion is that someone should make quite sure that he was not wearing coloured lenses . . . Oh, I think so . . . We'd be very glad to hear. It would make some things a bit clearer . . . Thank you. Goodbye.' He turned to me. 'Let's hope that takes the police off your back, Kate.'

How did he know they were on my back? 'And restores young Rex's confidence in his eyesight,' I added, trying to keep it light.

There were still two patient clients in the waiting-room. We did what we could for them and were clear by a quarter past one. I locked the office, while Jack helped the derelict Sam out into Wentworth Street, and bolted the door behind him. I hoped lunch would revive me, but it could take nothing off my mind.

IV

Maggie has lunch with us on Wednesdays. Our weekday lunches are usually soup, cheese and rolls—if you have some of the best Jewish bakers only a few doors away on either side, you might as well take full advantage of them. But Maggie insists on cooking on the days she comes to us. That's why Kevin always tries to get home on Wednesdays, and today he had managed it.

'H-hullo, Kate. I'm glad you did wake up in the end. Jack wouldn't let me call you. H-how's h-he doing in the C.A.B. ?'

'Better than me. He has a softer heart.'

'You're the first woman to recognize it, Kate.'

It was Maggie who looked at him suspiciously, and said, 'Come on now. Tell us what you've been up to.'

'I've accepted Lorraine as a temporary lodger—just for a week, to give them a break.'

'Who's Lorraine?'

'You h-haven't met h-her yet, Maggie. She's one of a very nice, h-hospitable commune we've just got to know.'

'Then why's she coming here?'

I looked at Jack, but he was pretending to be busy with his lunch, so I answered. I did not want to hold this difference in our judgement against him indefinitely.

'The man who died came from their commune, Maggie, so they're all pretty upset. As Jack says, they could do with a break.'

'I'll be surprised if she needs a break as much as you do, Kate.' Maggie's sympathetic care will, in the end, embrace everyone within range, but it takes time.

'She's not the one that needs the break,' said Jack rashly. I left him to placate Maggie, while I made us all some coffee. Usually we have tea at lunch-time, but I needed coffee today.

'Sh-she'll h-have Pam and Eric's sitting-room, I suppose. It will be splendid to be full again.' Kevin can find brightness in any situation. It was nice to have someone feel pleased.

Maggie insisted on cutting short her lunch break to go and get the room ready. She would not let me help.

'You're just to sit there and not move till two o'clock.

I'm not going to have you ill on my hands.'

'What nonsense, Maggie. I'm as well as you.'

'I wish you looked it.'

She stamped upstairs, and Kevin had to hurry back to work, so Jack and I were left looking at each other. I laughed.

'I suspect this is Maggie's way of telling you off, Jack.'

'And of looking after you, Kate. I'm glad to find some-one who's allowed to do it. No. You sit there, as she told you to, and if I do the washing-up, perhaps I can wheedle my way back into her good books.'

'There'll be no need for that. Maggie never bears grudges. She'll have forgotten all about it when she comes on Friday—always supposing that Lorraine behaves herself.'

'What a hope!' said Jack. But even hope proved un-necessary.

Back in the C.A.B., the third client Jack ushered in was Lorraine herself. She rushed up to me and I thought for a moment she was going to kiss me—a modern custom between comparative strangers, to which I am adjusting slowly—but she grasped my hand instead.

'Kate, that really is darling of you, to invite me here. I didn't know people could be so nice.' I could think of no unhurtful way of escaping this wholly undeserved appreciation, so I had to put up with the sense of un-worthiness it generated. 'I'd love to have come, and I hope you won't think it quite dreadfully ungrateful of me not to. But with Art dying like that, nothing's the same any more. There isn't any point in me staying on in London. I'll try out Margate again.'

'That's your home?'

'I suppose you could say so. That's where I'll go to begin with.'

'We're all dreadfully sorry about Art. I hadn't realized he mattered so much to you.'

'Nobody did.' Like Jill yesterday, I found her for once convincing. She was expressing a genuine emotion, but I

could not put a name to it, not grief—resentment perhaps.
'I tried to come earlier but you weren't in.'

'We had lunch very promptly—' but she was not
listening to me.

'I wanted to ask if you were really Mrs Ralph Weatherley,
Mrs Ralph Arthur Weatherley. And is your husband still
alive?' When I nodded, she said, 'Goodness! I'm glad
I'm not you,' and then fell silent, pondering, I thought,
the awfulness of my fate. Unexpectedly she added, 'Funny
boy Art—' she was eight or ten years younger than he had
been—'I never did understand him. But thanks for telling
me, and for the offer. Nice to have been able to kill two
birds with one stone.'

She was, I think, rising to go when the sound of a scuffle
in the waiting-room took Jack and me to the door. One
of the meths drinkers, who spend much of their shortened
lives in the bombed sites and churchyards round us, had
staggered into the room, dragged an empty chair towards
the fire and was trying to place it so close to the fire as to
exclude Sam. To my surprise, Sam, who had seemed particularly somnolent these last few days, was putting up
some resistance. The waiting clients, when I glanced
across at them to discover why they were taking no part,
proved to be not locals but strangers from the City, so
they were sitting very straight in their chairs, pretending
such things did not happen.

Jack took the chair from the newcomer and put it on
the other side of the fire from Sam, just as near the fire;
but this was of no use, and the meths drinker—poor bod,
he wasn't even old—staggered, mumbling and grumbling,
out of our door. We turned back to Lorraine.

She had come to the door and was fumbling in her bag
for a handkerchief, her nose wrinkled against the drinker's
pungent, pervasive smell. She was anxious to go, and all
she said was, 'Thanks again. 'Bye, Kate. 'Bye, Jack.'

We shut the door on the waiting-room. In the office,
the memory of Lorraine was more vivid than that of the
meths drinker.

'Do you understand her, Kate?'

'At all.' Such un-English idioms still linger from my West African childhood. 'There were two odd things—' The memory of the row of pained clients, waiting outside, stopped me. 'We'd better see the next, Jack.'

I was still seeing him—a straightforward case, wanting information on how to replace a lost passport—when there was again a commotion in the waiting-room. 'That meths drinker back again,' I said to Jack, and he went to investigate.

I was wrong. This time it was poor old Sam. He had, I suppose, been thoroughly upset by the previous incident, lost all hold on himself and slipped off his chair. He was struggling to pull himself up again, and I was glad to see that one of the waiting women was helping. He looked badly shaken, so I left him to Jack while I, with apologies to my passport case, fetched him some water from my desk. There was so little left in the jug—of course, being late that morning, I had forgotten to refill it—that it filled less than half the glass. I held it against Sam's shaky lips and managed to tip it all down his throat.

The water did not help at all. Sam spluttered and choked over it. His colour was worse than ever and he went rigid against Jack's supporting arms. He had never had a fit before. His breathing became laboured and extraordinarily noisy. I turned back to the office: 'I'll get an ambulance.'

I wasn't long—I know the number—but by the time I came back, Sam had turned the colour of grey clay and his breathing, from dominating the room, had become so faint you had to listen for it. Jack, very quiet, was still holding him. He looked absurdly small against Jack. The woman was fussing round, suggesting hot water bottles, blankets, more to drink—especially more to drink. It was a silly idea, with Sam unconscious, but I hated standing round doing nothing, so I took the jug and glass out to the kitchen—after all, one of us might need a drink, even if poor old Sam didn't.

I washed them both thoroughly, as I do every morning before I fill the jug—I never know who will have needed a drink from the glass—so by the time I carried the water back, the waiting-room was filling up. Perhaps the hawk-eyed Mrs Weinkopf from across the road had seen some excitement through the big window, or perhaps the fussy woman had gone to the door and called for help. I wouldn't put it past her.

'Mrs Weatherley, hadn't we better carry him out into the road? You know them ambulances won't collect anyone from a private house, not without a doctor's say-so.' Mrs Weinkopf knows everything.

'They'll take him.'

They did. I did not even have to argue with them that our waiting-room is a public place; Sam was so clearly in no state to be delayed or argued over. Jack went with Sam in the ambulance. Had he been conscious, I would have gone, to give him someone he knows. But he was in no state to know anybody.

## v

Jack was not back until soon after five. I had finished in the C.A.B., locked up, and come across into the empty kitchen. Maggie finishes at four, and on Wednesdays, Kevin goes straight from work to Toynbee Hall to help with one of their literacy classes.

Jack came in very quietly, and when I looked at his face I stopped getting out cups and sat down.

'Bad?'

'He's gone, Kate. He died in the ambulance. The ambulance men didn't even want to take him into the hospital, just get a doctor to come and certify him dead and go straight on to the mortuary. I wouldn't have that, the lazy—'

'It's not laziness. It's their instructions. If they can keep him out of the hospital, the hospital isn't responsible for burying him. But I'm glad you stopped that. An ambulance is no place to make sure. There's been at least one unexpected recovery in the mortuary.'

'Don't expect a recovery this time, Kate.'

'Of course not. Old Sam has been only half alive for years. I'll miss him all the same. It won't seem like our C.A.B.' The kettle was steaming noisily into the room, so Jack made the tea, while I went on thinking about Sam. 'Did they know at the London who he is, and that hostel where he lives? Ought we to be—?'

'It's all right, Kate. Elaine, one of your neighbours, came in the ambulance with us. She seemed to know everything.'

'She does. She's Mrs Weinkopf's daughter. You don't—'

We were interrupted—not for the last time that evening. It was my friend, Susan, whom I had rung the previous night. She looked rosy-cheeked, gay and relaxed. Most unusually, I found myself thinking with something like envy of the health and calmness one might find in the outer London suburbs. I introduced Jack to her.

'You must be her newest friend, and I'm her oldest.'

'You're not, Sue. You've forgotten that I still keep up with two school-friends.'

'Christmas-card friends! Anyway, I knew you before you were married, went to your wedding, and still hope to go to your divorce! We were at college together,' she explained to Jack. 'Yes, tea is exactly what I want, thank you. Your men here are always so handy,' she added, as Jack brought her tea, sugar, and even some biscuits which I didn't know we had. He seemed disinclined to talk so I concentrated on Sue.

'I mustn't stay long; Harry'll be looking out for me. But as I had to be in the city this afternoon I thought it would be more fun to bring you the fruits of my research, instead of talking remotely on the phone. It's not much, but I hope it's enough.'

She dug in her handbag, while I wondered whether I had meant to keep whatever information she had brought me private. But there was not much point in wondering, when neither she nor Jack had any thoughts of privacy.

'Here we are. You were quite right: Arthur is no longer this country's favourite name, *pace* the Round Table and all his knights. I covered all the London drug clinics, and even then I couldn't find more than eight registered addicts admitting to the name of Arthur. Most of those are the wrong age, but three seem to be in their thirties. So I dug into those three for all I was worth.' She broke off the tale to say to Jack, 'You can't imagine how little of my own work I've done today.'

'I can imagine very easily,' he said solemnly, playing up to her. He wasn't missing a word or an intonation.

She smiled at him sweetly and went on. 'We'd got to the three Arthurs, hadn't we? Well, two of them are definitely dark, one's probably a Cypriot or Greek or something Mediterranean. But the third is fair, thirty-one, long, straight, fair hair. Hasn't been registered more than eight or nine months, at one of the South London clinics. Lucky I threw my net so wide, and know there's more to London than East and West.'

She looked at the paper she had taken from her bag, gave me the name of the clinic, and went on: 'Anything else? Oh yes. He gave them an address and I looked it up and it doesn't seem to exist.'

I could not wait any longer and broke in. 'What about the name? But of course, that could be as false as the address.'

'Could be. Less likely, I should think. It's Smithson, Arthur Smithson. Any use?'

'I expect so. I think that must be the man we want. What do you think, Jack?'

'Could hardly be a better fit. Well done.' This was to me, not Sue. 'Perhaps we've got a thread to follow now. We'll out-do those police!'

'You've more than a thread. You've got your man bound hand and foot and handed to you on a platter. He's lying in the Charing Cross Hospital, just waiting for you, I expect. What's up with you two now? I thought I was giving you good news.'

'Alive or dead?' It didn't sound like my voice.

'Alive, of course. Once I'd got what looked like the right name, I thought I'd try some of the inner clinics again, in case they'd overlooked him or he had used only an initial with them. If junkies can wangle themselves on to more than one clinic's register, they do, of course. And when I gave the Charing Cross the name, Arthur Smithson, they said, "Arthur Smithson? He's one of our in-patients, in Men's Medical." They're quite small, you know, and can recognize names quicker than most. They wouldn't tell me what was wrong; that was against their regulations. But they told me his age and what he looked like and it's the same man. OK? I really must rush now. Sorry if it's not quite what you want.'

'You've done absolute marvels, Sue, and incredibly quickly. No, no. Don't worry. Shutting off false clues is as necessary as opening new ones.'

'We'll know where to come when we need anything more in this line,' said Jack. 'You've been terrific.'

But from someone who knows me as well as Susan, we could not really hide our disappointment that Arthur Smithson, the only relevant junkie she had found in a day's search of all the London drug clinics, was not, after all, the dead Art.

VI

I was on my way to show Susan out, when the telephone rang. Once the C.A.B. is closed, enquirers only too often ring the Settlement itself, especially if their enquiry is in the never-ending search for somewhere to sleep. We were lucky to have had no calls during Sue's visit, but such luck could not last all evening. I waved Sue off and went to the phone in the hall.

It wasn't a Settlement enquiry. It was Norman. And I

was foolish enough to say, 'Oh, Norman,' in a pleased
voice, while Sue was still standing with Jack in the kitchen
doorway. She had taken to Jack. She also likes Norman,
so she turned at once, said, 'Oh goodie! Give him my
love,' and settled down to listen unashamedly to the conversation. Perhaps after our years in college together, we
revert to that early post-adolescent stage when we're
together now. The only excuse for Jack settling down to
listen too was that nobody seemed in the least interested in
giving the call any sort of privacy.

So, with an interested audience of two, I received from
Norman details of the will that had had more influence
on my life than anything else I could think of at the
moment. I knew the most relevant parts, of course, though
it was curious to hear them repeated by someone who
had never even met Ralph.

He commented almost at once on my sounding low,
so I told him about Sam's death.

'I don't expect you remember him, Norman, in the
waiting-room, when I showed you the C.A.B. But he'll
have been there all right. He always is. I mean, he always
used to be. I can't imagine the place without him.'

Then we went on to the will. He said he had had a copy
made and would put it in the post to me, but were there
any details I wanted first.

'Just read the bits that look most relevant to Ralph
and me.'

He read quite a lot of it, all the part about Ralph's
annual allowance stopping when he was twenty-five,
unless he had already married an English spinster of
unsullied reputation—I had not known I had to be
English—in which case the allowance would continue for
ten years, after which he would inherit the very considerable capital. But this was dependent on his still
being married to the same wife. If, during the ten years,
there was a divorce or legal separation—it was an old
man who had left the will, sixteen years ago—the allowance would stop and the capital go to the Chancellor of

the Exchequer.

I said so little as I listened to this largely familiar recital, that Susan decided the waiting Harry was more important. She whispered, 'Goodbye,' and went. Jack had moved back into the kitchen, but the door was still open.

Norman had gone on to something I had not known. If Ralph were convicted of a felony at any time before he inherited the capital, the capital was to go absolutely to his wife. Rather oddly, as Norman permitted himself to comment, if the wife were similarly convicted, the capital would go at once to Ralph.

'And if they were convicted together?'

'We lawyers would have a particularly happy and profitable time.'

I was putting off asking the real question, the one the police had put into my mind. Subconsciously perhaps I was hoping that the kitchen door would be shut before we reached that point. It remained open and I went on:

'And what happens if either of them dies before the ten years are up?'

'Just the same as in the case of a felony. If either dies, all the money goes at once to the other. But, of course, in this case the law is clear, if they both died together, in a car smash for instance, it would be assumed that the elder had died first and the money would go to the heirs of the younger. That's a well-established—'

I did not hear any more. There had been a knocking at the door, Jack had gone to answer it, and of the four men I could glimpse on our steps, two wore police uniform.

'Thank you very much, Norman. Someone's just called. I'll have to go.'

I managed to hang up before Inspector Brownfield could take the receiver out of my hand. I took the offensive.

'I was just ringing a solicitor friend. Do come and sit down.'

'You had decided this was the time to ring your solicitor?'

'I don't have a solicitor. This is a friend who happens
to be a solicitor, Mr Norman Conroy.'

'And if you were in trouble and needed a solicitor,
perhaps Mr Conroy is the man you'd call.'

'Perhaps he is.'

They were as hostile as ever, and I was not sure I had
the energy for fighting. Jack had sat down in the kitchen
with us all, and no one had asked him to go away.

'We've come about the death of Mr Parkinson.'

'Oh, you've found his name. I'm so glad. Now you
know he's not Mr Weatherley.'

'I don't think we're talking about the same man, Mrs
Weatherley. We're talking about Mr Samuel Parkinson,
who died in your Citizens' Advice Bureau this afternoon.'

'Of course, poor old Sam—'

'You know he died of poison, Mrs Weatherley?'

'Poison? How dreadful!' They were all sitting silent
now, waiting for me to go on. 'We'd thought it was some
sort of collapse. He'd been upset by a meths drinker a bit
earlier. But when did he take it? He wouldn't mean to.'

'Nobody suggests he meant to, Mrs Weatherley. We
suggest it was in the drink you gave him. It was a quick-
acting poison; it must have been taken shortly before his
death. Is there anything you want to say, Mrs Weatherley?
I should warn you—'

I listened to the standard warning. It was one of the
plainclothes men who had taken over, and he added that
he might have warned me a bit early, but that was better
than too late. There was nothing I wanted to say. I could
feel myself pouring that half glass of water down Sam's
throat, while he spluttered and choked. And it was poison
I had been giving him. Where had that come from? No.
There was, I found, plenty I wanted to say.

'I gave Sam half a glass of water from the jug on my
desk. How was that poisoned?'

'We'd like to see the room and the jug and glass.'

We trooped into the empty waiting-room and crowded
into the door of my little office. The jug, full of water,

and the clean, empty glass stood shining on my desk.

The detective looked at them doubtfully. 'These are the ones? Have they been used since?'

'I gave him all there was in the jug. It hadn't been filled this morning.' I sat down wearily. There seemed such a lot to explain. 'I was late this morning, so I didn't see to the jug or anything. Then, when I'd given all there was to Sam, I went back to the kitchen for more. One of the women who was trying to help kept asking for more water.'

'You brought out the jug and just filled that?'

'I suppose so. No. I brought them both. I remember washing them both out.'

'You came in here and washed them both out, while Mr Parkinson was lying next door, dying?'

'I didn't know he was dying. I wash them both out every day, and as I hadn't done it before, I did it then. There was nothing I could do for Sam. People were looking after him, and I'd rung for the ambulance.'

'Inspector'—they all looked round at Jack, of whom they had hitherto seemed unaware—'if the poison was in the jug, as you are supposing, it must have been meant for someone other than Sam Parkinson. Nobody could know he was going to fall off his chair, and need a drink. His getting it must have been an accident. Who was it really meant for?'

'You can get too clever and miss what's right under your nose.' The detective sounded almost affable in his account of the right approach to detection. 'Here we've got two men dead in three days, one just outside the house and one inside it. And Mrs Weatherley was closely connected, very closely connected, with one, and gave the poison to the other. *And* washed the glass and jug out immediately afterwards. We've got to take it seriously.'

The four police moved into the waiting-room for a very quiet consultation. *They* knew how to get privacy when they wanted it. Jack stayed unspeaking in the doorway, watching them and me. They were not long.

'We'll be going now. We'll take the jug and glass with us.' They carried them out, water and all. 'You won't be going away at all, Mrs Weatherley?'

'No. I shall be here.'

I stayed in my chair, leaving Jack to show them out. He took them to the big swing door, and as he straightened up from unbolting it, he said: 'Any news of the junkie?'

It was Inspector Brownfield who answered, a little grudgingly, I thought. 'We find he'd registered under the name of Arthur Smithson, at a clinic across the river. Needn't be his right name, of course.'

'But you're sure it was the right man?'

'Quite sure, Mr Winters. One of the nurses from the clinic came up to the mortuary and identified him for us. She was quite certain—just like that bunch of squatters were when they identified him. He hadn't given their address—just a made-up one.'

'Perhaps he registered before he moved there.'

'That might be. Two or three months before. But they're still meant to notify any change of address, and not give false ones. Now we've still got no clear relatives.'

'And did you follow up our suggestion about the lenses?'

He was more grudging than ever and they all went as soon as he'd answered.

'Yes. It turns out he was wearing brown lenses over blue eyes.'

VII

'So they'll have to give up thinking Art was your husband.' Jack had bolted the door behind the four police, had come back to find me still sitting in my office, and had sat down opposite me. 'They'll have to accept that you were right in thinking the dead Art and your client were the same man. And they'll have to accept that you and young Rex can recognize a blue eye when you see it.

We're making progress.'

But he wasn't making much progress in shaking me out of my heaviness. I was suppressing the memory of me, pouring poison down the spluttering Sam's throat. I tried to rouse myself.

'They've already refused to believe that I could identify Ralph. They won't believe for a moment that he has brown eyes.'

'You could bring Susan in to confirm it.'

'Why should they believe one of my oldest friends— doubtless most anxious to help keep me out of trouble?'

'Perhaps now they've got a name, some Smithson relations will turn up.'

'Perhaps the other Arthur Smithson is one of the relations.'

'A constructive suggestion, Kate. Does that mean you're coming to? What would you like to do now? Go to bed and let me bring you up some supper? When do we expect Kevin home?'

'He never knows on a Wednesday. I'm not a bit hungry. A hot drink is all I want, I think. But there's no need at all for you to bring it up to me. What are you going to eat? Let's go and see to it.'

So we locked the C.A.B. up again and went back to the kitchen, where Jack insisted on making me some cheese and chutney sandwiches to take upstairs with my hot milk. He said he would wait a little while to see if Kevin came in for supper too, and added: 'If your light is still on, I'll look in on my way upstairs to see if you want anything else.'

I heard Kevin come in soon after I was in bed. They must have had a quick supper, because Kevin came up to his room, beside mine, not long afterwards. The food had done me good and I decided that when Jack came I would ask him for something more—fruit perhaps. I lay listening for him, but when he came upstairs, he only paused very briefly on our landing before going on up to his own room.

I was ridiculously disappointed. I put on my dressing-gown and slippers, crept downstairs—I did not want Jack or Kevin to hear me—ate a banana, and drank some more milk—cold this time. I felt no better. It was not food I wanted but company and Jack had let me down.

I went upstairs again. There was no light under my door, but when I opened it, I realized that the bedside lamp, which was all I had had on since getting into bed and which was still on, does not shine under the door, as the central lamp does. And I had been blaming Jack!

I went up the next flight of stairs to explain to him. The door of his little room was open and he was sitting writing at the table. He jumped up when he saw me—I was in soft slippers and none of our stairs creak.

'I've come to explain that I hadn't really turned my light out. I hadn't realized that the bedside lamp doesn't shine under the door.'

'And you want some more supper. Good. What can I get you?'

'Thank you. I've been down and got it for myself, thinking most unfairly that you had deserted me. Perhaps I've really come to apologize for my unfair thoughts.'

'That's very handsome of you. Do you feel more like talking now? We seem to be in the middle of so many conversations. I should like to finish some of them. Let's go into the front room, the one Lorraine doesn't want after all, and light the gas fire, and talk comfortably.'

Pam and Eric's sitting-room is not as elegant as Agnes's, nor as comfortable as my bed-sitter, which is sandwiched between them. But those three big front rooms above the waiting-room are the nicest in the house and the only ones with gas fires. Jack pulled up Eric's big armchair and I snuggled into that, while he sat on a low stool, leaning against the wall beside the fire. I had grown used to his looking at me and decided that he probably did it to anyone he was talking to—part of his total concentration on whatever he is doing at any moment.

'Did you tell Kevin about Sam?'

'Yes, indeed. He was really flattened by it. He's a very soft-hearted bloke, Kevin, much kinder, Kate, than I am.'

'Is he? Perhaps. Not many people are as kind as Kevin. Did he have any ideas on who had done it or why?'

'He didn't stay to talk. He just went up to his room, to grieve, I think.'

'Poor old Kevin.' But we weren't there ourselves just to grieve, so I asked, 'Which conversations did we leave in the air?'

He replied promptly, 'The one about Lorraine for one. You were saying there were two odd things about her.' You can't withdraw or forget anything you have once said to Jack, but you can throw it back at him.

'Yes. What did *you* think odd?'

'The oddest thing, surely, was her saying there was no point in her staying on in London now Art was dead. And the others tell us that she and Art never spoke.'

'There was obviously quite a lot between them, on some level. She implied that herself, didn't she?'

'What did you see as the other oddity?'

It was my turn. 'What did she mean by killing two birds with one stone? One was thanking us for the offer, and refusing it. The only other thing she did was ask about my being Mrs Weatherley and if Ralph was still alive. What importance could that have to her?'

'Unless she meant something quite, quite different, like putting poison in the water jug.' I sat silent and he went on, 'However crazy it sounds, somebody must have done that.'

'Oh, I know. And if we could once find out who, the police would leave me alone. So I've been thinking who had an opportunity, and the list seems endless—in my carefully locked room! Me first, of course, as the police point out.'

'And me next. I went in on my own this morning, remember.'

'Did Kevin go in with you? No, of course, he'd gone to work already.'

'And yours is the only key? Well, then there's Lorraine. We left her alone in your office, when we went out to the meths drinker.'

'We left someone else alone in the room, when we first went out to Sam, before I went back for the glass of water —what I thought was water. Who on earth was it? Oh, that passport case. I've never seen him before or since. Unless he's a total lunatic, and the whole poisoning has no logic at all, and has no connection with Art and Ralph, I'd put him at the very bottom of my list.'

'He had a wife sitting waiting for him in the waiting-room. I think that cuts him out. The list is certainly long enough without him, Kate. As you didn't wash the jug this morning, do we have to include anyone who had a chance yesterday too?'

'Not during office hours. Don't you remember I was drinking water until you brought us in the tea?'

'So you were. But then in the evening—'

'Jill, and Rex, and Sheila—no, not Sheila. She never came into my office but we took both the others in last night.'

'And Kevin then too.'

'But, Jack, we didn't leave them alone, not like Lorraine this morning.'

'I've been thinking about that. I know we never left them alone, but it wasn't at all as if they were clients, sitting still in a chair. We were all standing and moving about, and turning our backs to get out books. If one of them had wanted to, I think they could have poisoned the water quite easily.'

'I suppose so, especially if they were in it together. I find it very hard to imagine of Jill. I really don't believe she could. Under that elfish appearance, she's a motherly person.'

'But you don't rule out Rex? I agree with you, Kate. And what about Tim this morning? Did he have a chance?'

'No. He just sat in the chair, like a client. And the

water is right the other end of the desk. You saw him.'

'Yes. I'd rule him out too, Kate. We've plenty without him.'

'That's not the end of the list. Don't you remember, we were talking so hard when we went to coffee that between us we never locked the office and there were two people waiting in it, when we got back, weren't there? I know them both, and for myself, I'd count them out at once. But someone else might have slipped in and out again.'

'That was my fault, Kate. I had the key. That leaves the list wide open.'

'Not quite. We have our spies. I'll go and see Mrs Weinkopf in the morning. She's the one with the shoe shop opposite us, across Wentworth Street, and she sits outside it all day and sees everyone that comes into our waiting-room and nearly everything that goes on inside.'

'Elaine's mother. I remember. She knows everything.'

'Exactly. She'll know who went in during our coffee break, and she'll tell me. If it was someone local, they'd probably come back later, because they'd know they'd be seen and it would look funny never to come back. Even a non-local might think of that. I'll ask Ma Weinkopf if anyone came twice yesterday, and as well if anyone went in during the coffee break and never came back again.'

'You do have a useful network, Kate. Then we'll be able to complete our list of the few dozen people who had an opportunity to poison the water. What about motive?'

'It all depends on who was meant to be killed. Let's start by supposing it really was poor old Sam. Then a possible motive would be to implicate me. I didn't tell you, Jack, that when the police came for the second time yesterday, the time they followed you into this side of the house and came up to Agnes's room, they were trying to suggest that I'd want Ralph dead, that I'd tried to kill him, and they said they were acting on "information received". If someone is trying to smirch me, for some extraordinary reason, I suppose they might even go to the length of poisoning Sam. Perhaps they wouldn't know the poison was as strong as it proved to be.'

Jack went on looking at me for some time before he said: 'And who would want to implicate you so badly, Kate, and for what reason?' The silence stretched itself out before he added, 'The will says something about criminal convictions.'

I took a deep breath and said pretty ungraciously, 'I think I've got to spread it all out in front of someone and I guess it might as well be you.' Most people would, I think, have protested that I must not tell them anything I did not really want to. Characteristically, Jack merely sat and waited. He had to wait quite a time. I wanted to bring out into the air everything relevant about my marriage. And it was many years since I had talked to anyone about Ralph.


## VIII


I started at last, curled in the big chair, looking at the steady flames of the gas fire, while Jack leant back against the wall and watched me.

'You'd need to have known Ralph ten, eleven years ago, to get a proper picture of him. He wasn't an undergraduate like the rest of us that he went about with. He was taking some unimportant, outside course, and somehow we all felt he didn't need to bother with degrees. He has enormous charm—not just spurious charm—you mustn't think that. He has this ability to make anyone he talks to feel they are the cleverest and most important person in the world—and if you are a woman, the most amazingly beautiful too. He gives all his attention to whoever he's with—rather like you do, Jack. It never struck me before, but really you're rather like him, in lots of ways. Funny I never noticed—perhaps I did subconsciously and it's made me rather, well, careful towards you.'

I waited for Jack's response, but he only said, 'Go on

about Ralph, Kate.'

I took another deep breath and went on.

'He had lots and lots of money, and much more spare time than most of us, and he went about with many more different groups. We always thought he was mostly with ours, so we were rather surprised, when we came back from our last long vacation, to find he'd got engaged to a girl from quite another set that we didn't see much of. She was a very pretty, lively little thing, but given to black moods. I suppose it's rather funny,' I added drearily, 'that I was one of the very few people—I'd been with her a lot right at the beginning, when we were both freshers— who knew that she'd been married, very young, almost the moment she'd left her snob school, and her husband had been killed in a smash on their honeymoon. It was after that that she decided to go to university, as her school had always wanted, and she went back to her maiden name, and her parents came up and visited her, like most people's did, and most of even her close friends had no idea she'd ever been married. But no wonder she had those black moods. We all thought it was due to them that the engagement didn't last. It ended suddenly after only a week or so, and they both avoided each other like the plague ever afterwards.'

I fell silent, thinking about pretty, unhappy little Celia and hoping life had treated her well in the end. 'Susan heard that she got married about three years later, so I hope that was good.'

Jack was so silent that, had it not been for his eyes, I might have thought him asleep. 'Does all this bore you?'

'God, no, Kate. It wouldn't make it any easier if I kept butting in, would it? I thought you might prefer to forget me and think you were talking to yourself.'

'I'll try, thank you.' But he's not an easy man to forget. 'Anyway, quite soon after that, after the engagement ended, Ralph turned to me. I thought heaven had fallen into my lap. I tried to put off a public engagement for as long as possible, so as not to hurt Celia, the earlier

fiancée. But it became so obvious, that there wasn't much
point and we announced it when we came back after
Christmas. There was only one major difference after that.'

Jack stopped pretending not to be there and said: 'He
wanted to sleep with you, and being the puritan you are,
you wouldn't.'

I was really surprised. 'I've never known you wrong
before, Jack, but you're totally out this time. It was just
the opposite. Once we were engaged I think I'd have done
anything he asked. I don't know. What did well brought
up girls of twenty do ten years ago?'

'The same as they do now, but less openly.'

'I suppose so. But Ralph didn't want to. I was surprised—I think secretly rather hurt that he didn't want
to. All he wanted was to get married as quickly as possible.
That was where we differed. My mother—she was terribly
pleased about the engagement, though she hadn't yet met
Ralph—was already ill. She died the following winter.
My father's married again. I've a really nice step-mother.
They're out in the States.' Perhaps I welcomed the opportunity to stop talking about my marriage.

'I'm sorry, Kate. I thought you seemed not to have
much family about.'

'I've a brother as well and a sister-in-law and two
nephews, but their home is in Ghana again. That was
where my father had been teaching for years, but because
of Mother's illness, they were coming home for good in
the summer, as soon as the school term ended. They
wanted to be at my wedding, of course, and I was longing
to have them there. And Ralph wouldn't wait. He just
wouldn't wait. Trying to please me, he suggested a secret
registrar's office wedding, and then a big ceremony when
they arrived. But I wouldn't have that. I didn't want a big
ceremony—Quakers don't. I wanted my parents at the
real wedding. Then he said'—I hadn't meant to tell
anyone this, but I found myself embarked on it—'that he
just couldn't stand waiting for me any longer, that it was
driving him demented, that he had principles against sex

before marriage, but that having to go on waiting—' I
found I was trembling, just at the memory of those long-
ago battles. When I could trust my voice again, I went on.

'I couldn't hold out against that, so I gave in and we
were married in early June, almost ten years ago. My
parents were very sweet about it. My mother died while
the marriage still seemed a gay, happy affair. I've sometimes been glad that she wasn't still here to see the
marriage end, but I think I've been wrong. She could
have taken the truth and somehow found it good. She
always could—even dying.'

'You've been lucky.'

'This is a *sad* saga!'

'Of course. But you've been lucky in your parents.'

'Goodness, yes. Let's get this interminable story finished.
I'm sorry I've made the preliminaries so long. We had
ten pretty good months. I don't know whether Ralph was
ever much in love with me—I was so much in love with
him and so overwhelmed at his choosing to marry me. But
I think perhaps he was for a time. Then, after Mother
died, I had to go and help my father for a few weeks, and
when I got back I found he'd had another woman to stay
with him—in our home. I forgave him—I'd have forgiven
him almost anything—but I protested first, and he, he
just laughed. He said we each might as well get used to
what the other was like, because we'd got to put up with
each other for ten years, "come rain or shine". I said, "But
Ralph, we've married each other for life," and he said,
"But it's the first ten years that count, if we're not going
to be paupers." That was when he first told me about his
grandfather's will.'

Jack, to prompt me out of the silence into which I had
again relapsed, said, 'That's the will you were listening to
on the phone?'

'Yes. Old Grandfather Bloxham was an exceedingly
wealthy man, who had an only child, Ralph's mother.
She'd married a charming wastrel, who had left her soon
after their only child, Ralph, was born. The old man was

terrified that Ralph, his grandson, would take after his
father. So when his daughter died, without marrying
again, as old Bloxham had always hoped, and Ralph was
left as his only descendant, he drew up a will trying to
save anyone else's daughter from the same fate as his own.
Ralph was to lose his big, monthly allowance if his
marriage ended during its first ten years, and to get all the
capital if it lasted so long. Ralph managed to make me
laugh about it too, and I said, laughing at so absurd a
joke, "I promise, however bad you are, I won't divorce
you for at least ten years," and he said, "I'll hold you to
that, Kit," and we both laughed a lot. I almost managed
to put the other girl he had had there out of my mind,
and we went on much as before for some weeks, with
threats of divorce a standing joke between us.'

Wholly absorbed in my memories, I needed no prompt-
ing now.

'If Ralph had never told me any more of the will than
that, I suppose we might still be together, even if I'd had
to accept his having other girls, if ever I had to go away,
anyway. But once he'd started telling me about the will,
it must have stayed in his mind. It wasn't very long afterwards, one night in bed, he said to me something about,
"If I'd had any idea what fun you'd be in bed, Kit, I don't
think I'd have waited those months of our engagement,
whatever the risk." And I said, "What risk? I've long
stopped believing in your principles against premarital
sex." And Ralph laughed and said, "I should hope so.
It was such a thin story, I hardly thought you'd believe it
then."' I fell silent again, and it was as well that Jack
made no attempt to prompt me. I was talking to myself,
and might have stopped, if reminded that I had a listener.

'Ralph said, "The will said that to keep the money, I
had to be married before my twenty-fifth birthday, to
a spinster of unsullied reputation. If I'd let myself
sleep with you before we were married, someone might
have found out and blackmailed me ever afterwards. That
was the risk, but I almost think I was silly not to take it.

What do you think, Kit?" He started pulling me towards him again, but I broke away and sat up in the dark, and said, "That's why we had to be married in June, before your birthday?" and he said, "Of course," and I went on, "Because of the money, nothing to do with not being able to wait for me." And he said, "Not then, Kit, it's now I can't wait for you." I said, "You broke it off with Celia, when she told you she was a widow. Otherwise you'd be married to her now." He said, "Sure I would. So isn't it lucky for you that she was a widow—" and I climbed out of bed, and put on the light, and dressed, and walked out.'

Jack let the silence lengthen again, but after a time I remembered him and said apologetically, 'I've nearly finished. Ralph tried quite hard to persuade me to stay: cajolery, threats, ridicule, even pleas. But too much had been destroyed, trust and pride, all my confidence in myself as well as in him. Some came back slowly, when I found my heart wasn't totally broken. I saw Ralph now and then at first, mostly meeting to divide up our possessions, and we exchanged cards at Christmas for four or five years. But I haven't his present address. I tried the solicitor, Grandfather Bloxham's solicitor, this morning, but he has no address now, just gets a phone message once a month telling him where to send a money order for the monthly allowance.'

'He's sure it's really Ralph phoning?'

'Oh yes. He knows Ralph and Ralph's voice well. It's odd all the same—so unlike Ralph. But it will all be over next June.'

'That's the ten years? That's the end of your promise? That's when you'll be free?'

'That's it. That's when Ralph at last inherits his fortune.'

'And where does being convicted come in?'

'I'm impossible! That's what this whole long tale was meant to be making clear to you, wasn't it? But everything has been stirred up again these last few days and I had to tell someone, Jack. I'm grateful to you for listening so courteously.'

He tried to say something, but seemed for once at a loss for words, so I carried on:

'The conviction. Norman, a solicitor friend of mine, who's just looked out the will for me, tells me—I hadn't known that part of the will before—that if either Ralph or I is convicted of a felony during these ten years—or if either of us dies for that matter—the whole of the inheritance goes at once to the remaining one. If it weren't that June's only four months away—and even then, I suppose, if he had some really desperate need of money— you could say that this gives Ralph a motive for incriminating me.'

'Or for murdering you.'

'I didn't say I'd married a monster!'

'Some people would do anything for money.'

'Ralph would do a lot—as you can see. But marrying for money is not the same as murdering for money.'

'I'm not sure it isn't worse.'

He looked so mutinous, I had to laugh at him. 'Jack, you do exaggerate. And you do do me good. I feel as if I'd thrown off an enormous weight. I hope it hasn't landed plonk on you and crushed you.' I looked at him solicitously and he managed a not very spontaneous smile. 'I'm sure you'd bounce back again. Do you know, I think I could sleep now. I don't want to work out motives or anything till I've got a clear head tomorrow morning. I'll thank you properly then too for putting up with me and all my troubles half the night.'

He came down to the half-landing, so that he could see me go safely into my room. We were very quiet, so as not to disturb Kevin—but nothing disturbs Kevin. I waved to Jack from my door, shut it, hung up my dressing-gown, dropped off my slippers, and fell into bed. Something had been exorcized: I slept where I fell, dreamlessly, all night.

# THURSDAY, 17 FEBRUARY

## I

I WOKE on Thursday feeling somehow younger, more clear-headed and unburdened than I had for days. I rolled on to my back and tried to think why. The realization that I had told the most private part of my life history to Jack, after keeping it to myself for nearly ten years, shocked me—would we be able to meet without embarrassment?—but did not destroy my sense of renewed well-being.

I did not intend to start just then working at our unsolved problems. I had a feeling that I would work them out better with Jack, though I recognized this as irrational. He had a good mind, but no special skill at detection, and, I had to remind myself, he was still a stranger. He now knew a great deal about me, but I still knew practically nothing about him. I must correct that.

One new piece of the problem surfaced in my mind and would not be pushed down again. It was the second Arthur Smithson, the one lying alive in Charing Cross Hospital. Just when we thought we had disposed of doubles, when we had satisfied ourselves that the blue-eyed client, claiming to be Ralph, and the brown-eyed junkie, dead in our gutter, and the ambivalent-eyed Art, from Romford Street, were all one and the same dead Arthur Smithson, here was another Arthur Smithson. He was the same age and had the same looks but was still alive, so he had to be recognized as a separate entity, a true double.

'Zarathustra, that great king, my daughter,
   Met his own self, walking in the garden.'
I shivered.

I thought for a long time about the live Arthur Smithson. I hoped he had brown eyes. I would ring Charing Cross Hospital at some decent hour in the morning.

The house still seemed quiet as I dressed and went downstairs, but when I reached the lower flight, I heard Jack in the kitchen. He was singing more softly than he had done on other days:

'Oh, I could be a banker,
And a right good banker I'd be,
But the very thought of—'

He stopped as I went in, and looked at me as usual, with no new constraint, thank goodness. So I was able to smile at him and say:

'Are you a banker, Jack, masquerading as a hobo?'

'No, Kate. I'm an unemployed lecturer, which is the next best thing to a hobo today. Funnily enough, my mother wanted me to be a banker, naturally in one of the small, distinguished private banks.'

'And couldn't she wangle it?'

'My mother can wangle anything, except me. I declined. After watching her use her wealth to crush my father and distort the whole family, not excluding herself, poor old thing, I had no wish to spend my life handling money.' He added, 'Perhaps my father wasn't quite crushed. It was he who taught me the Hobo Song.'

'But your mother is allowed to support you, and pay your alimony?' I am not usually so discourteously aggressive; perhaps I was getting my own back for last night's confidences.

He laughed at me. 'No alimony, Kate.' Then he was abruptly serious again. 'My wife died in childbirth three years ago. The baby died too. Don't say you're sorry, Kate. Remember your mother who could find good in any truth, even dying.'

'I'll try,' I said, but he knew I was feeling desperately sorry for him, and he smiled and said:

'Thank you. As to my financial arrangements—'

'You know you don't need to tell me!'

'I save when I'm earning, and so far that's been adequate. I've got a temporary job for the term after Easter.'

'That's good. But I am glad you're here now, and I'm terribly grateful for your patience last night.'

Once more he said nothing, but at least I had tried to clear my debts.

None of us eat big breakfasts, so we had finished and were taking the plates to the sink when Kevin at last rushed in, accepted nothing but a cup of tea, with which he nearly scalded himself, and departed to his office. I asked Jack to open up the C.A.B. and start on the first client, while I went across the road to speak to Mrs Weinkopf.

It was another fine morning, so the stalls were up out-side the shops. Jake was in charge of Mrs Weinkopf's stall, and Elaine of the shop, while the little crippled Bertie sat in a push-chair beside Mrs Weinkopf. She likes best to sit in the shop porch, but when the stall is up, she has to move further out if she is not to lose sight of our C.A.B. entrance. I was glad to see that she was keeping up her interest and had made sure of a clear view.

Our preliminary exchanges had to be longer than usual. Apart from enquiries as to the health of her own family, and of our absent Residents, there was the life and death of poor old Sam to be mulled over, before we even touched on the sad but well-deserved fate of the 'Russian spy'.

'We all feel that he got what he asked for, young as he was. Have the police put a name to him yet?—Not that it will be his own.'

I hope I gave nothing away, but for once I learnt nothing either, until I turned more directly to what I wanted to know.

'What with these deaths, Mrs Weinkopf, things aren't quite as straight as I like them to be, and—'

'And I'm sure that student you've taken on'—Jack's status had been determined in the Lane, beyond argument—'he won't keep your books the way you do your-self. Not but what you'll teach him,' she added hand-somely.

With this useful misunderstanding as to what I meant by 'straight', I was able to go easily on. 'I thought you'd be able to remind me about the people who went into the C.A.B. yesterday. Was there anybody went in twice?'

'Twice? Yes. Now, there were that young woman, the little blonde one that came back early in the afternoon. She must've been the second or third you saw.'

'I know. She told me she'd tried earlier and had to come back. She can't have realized that we shut for lunch when we can.'

'Lunch? Did she have the nerve to say it were the lunch-hour when she were there first?' I thought about that and decided Lorraine had not. That had been my own gloss. 'She weren't anywhere round during your lunch-hour. It were much earlier she were there. You and that student, you took your coffee break yesterday earlier than what you do most days and that were when she come. Just slipped inside she did, and when she found no one there, she come straight out and I don't know where she went. I didn't see her again till she come back after lunch. But she's in there again this morning. About the second to go in she were.'

'She's in there now, Mrs Weinkopf? I do want to see her. I'll go straight back and not leave her to Mr Winters. Thank you very much for your help.'

'You know we're all pleased when we can help you, Mrs Weatherley. There's a lot more than that I can tell you, when you've the time.' I appreciated her being con-siderate of my time for once. There is no end to what Mrs Weinkopf could tell me.

I went straight into our waiting-room from Wentworth Street, and with my mind on Lorraine, was ready automatically to say a cheerful word to old Sam as I passed him. His empty chair, still in its usual place by the gas fire, shocked me into remembering that I could never do anything for him again. I might help find his murderer, but that could do nothing for Sam. I carry no torch for revenge.

Lorraine was already with Jack in my office. I was sorry not to have forestalled her. I should like to have had a chance to tell Jack that Lorraine must be added to our list of those with the opportunity to poison my water. No. She was already on our list. But she was the only one, apart from Jack and me, with more than one opportunity.

Jack moved out of my chair and said: 'Lorraine was visiting Tim, where he works, so she kindly came across at the same time to say goodbye, as she goes to Margate tomorrow.'

'And to ask about the old man,' put in Lorraine, with more openness than I had expected of her. 'Tim told me he'd collapsed after that to-do with the meths drinker.' I was just going to ask how Tim knew—it had happened long after he had been in the office—when I remembered that he works locally.

'He died in the ambulance.' Jack was leaving it to me.

'Oh! That's awful! He wasn't really knocked about by the other man, was he? He must have been on his last legs to be finished by that. Poor bloke.'

She did not sound in the least like a poisoner. But then Lorraine had rarely sounded very real anyway, so how could one judge?

'He'd been on his last legs for a long time. Thank you for coming in again. I'm sorry you had to come back yesterday afternoon after being here so early in the morning.'

'That was all right. I had quite a bit of shopping I wanted to do round here before I go. And then when I saw Tim, he told me about your offering to put me up, so I had to come back.'

'Then what was it you came for the first time?'

'Just to ask about you being Mrs Ralph Weatherley. It seemed so funny with Art pretending that was his name. I'd have liked to get to the bottom of it before I went.'

'So would we, Lorraine.'

'I bet!'

If this was the last time we were to see her, I might as well push hard.

'Lorraine, you must know some things we don't and we may know some things you don't, so perhaps between us we could get to the bottom of it. Did you know his real name?'

She had leant forward most encouragingly at my first suggestion, the blue eyes in her little, heavily made-up face almost sparkling, but she withdrew at once at my question.

'No. I can't tell you that. That's just what I promised him I wouldn't.'

Where should I go from there? 'The police say it's Arthur Smithson.'

'They've got that, have they? Then that's the end of that promise. They're quite right. But it's not my name any more. I've been married.'

I was thrown into silence by the unexpectedness of her last remarks. Jack was quicker and took over.

'You're Art's sister?'

'That's right.'

'Then we must be able to sort this out between us. How was it you were both living in Romford Street?'

'I don't know how it was Art went there. He never told me. He was six years older than me, you know, and never told me much, though he used to stick up for me, when we were little. You got a brother?' she threw at me suddenly.

'Yes, only two years older than me.'

'That must have been nice. But Art always used to help me out if I was in a jam. So when I ran into him in London, just the end of the summer, and found him so flush, I decided I'd better stick around.' She fell silent, thinking, and then said more slowly, 'He wouldn't give me a peep as to where his money was coming from, but it was coming all right. I've never known him so loaded, and a junkie with it. They never have two pennies to rub together.'

Jack and I were very quiet, frightened that any interruption might stop these welcome reminiscences.

'So I managed to move in with him, into the same squat, and he passed some of the money over when I needed it. I'm not greedy,' she added defensively, 'I don't want more than enough. Enough is enough is enough.'

The memory of Art's support had cheered her, and she went on happily, giving me no time to muse on that useful word 'enough'.

'Jill is awfully nice, and Sheila's not bad, and I have my own boy-friend, as you know'—she looked sideways at Jack; did he know?—'so I haven't seen much of the men. It wasn't a bad place to be. But Art got more and more screwed up. He'd often been depressed, but this wasn't the same. It was more as if he was trying to key himself up to something. Of course, it's not easy to tell with a user, but I know him pretty well, and as I saw it, he was being pushed bloody hard about something. Get the feeling?'

We nodded hastily and she carried straight on:

'I reckoned he ought to tell me what it was all about, and I might have been able to help, and between us we could have been sure of keeping the money flowing in. But he wouldn't drop a hint, just swore me to secrecy about his starting to use that silly false name. Sorry. Of course, it's your husband's name, but it sounded awfully silly when you knew his real name was Art Smithson.'

I smiled forgiveness at her, but she was not stopping.

'So I decided it was time I put on a bit of pressure myself, in hopes of getting him to let me in on whatever it was, before it all dried up. With Art getting so jumpy, I was afraid that was what was going to happen. And was I right! So first I said I was going to move my boy-friend in too, and if they didn't let me, I'd blow the gaff on his false name, promise or no promise. My boy-friend wouldn't have come, so perhaps it was a silly thing to think up.'

She brooded on that, until I said, 'How did Art react?'

'First he said he didn't think the others would take it. Then when I offered to call it off if he'd let me in on the deal, he stopped saying anything. So it didn't work. And he was right about the others being dead against it. Jill and Rex made all sorts of plans to stop it, even wanted to move me out, out of a *commune*, where you're all meant to stick together!'

'And the other two?'

'Sheila and Tim stood up to Jill and Rex about it, quite friendly. I was really surprised.'

'And did you manage to find out anything from Art?'

She looked at me sideways then, moving her eyes without moving her head, and suddenly I wondered whether she was making the whole thing up, or parts of it, or whether we had any grounds for believing her at all. She said:

'Nothing. Not a bloody thing. And what about you? Have you found out anything?'

It was difficult to think what we had to give her, to balance her contribution—if it was true.

'We've not got very far. His name, and the clinic over near the Elephant, where he was getting his dope.'

'That's where he used to live.'

'And about his lenses. He was wearing brown-coloured lenses over his eyes, which you know were blue like yours.'

Of course, that was who she had reminded me of when I had first met her at the party, the impostor client that I had been dwelling on so much that very day. Perhaps she was telling the truth.

'Yes. I knew about those lenses. He'd only had them a day or two. They came some time the week before he died.' No wonder he had not been wearing them when he came to the C.A.B. 'He got me to try and help him put them in and take them out. He didn't find them easy. I never knew what he wanted them for.'

She stood up. 'Well, between us we don't seem to have sussed out much. I don't suppose we ever will now, and what does it matter? Art's gone.'

I said, 'I am really sorry about Art. Have you any other brothers and sisters?'

'Sisters. I'm going down to tell them about Art now.'

'And everything all right with your boy-friend?'

She smiled across at Jack. It's not many girls who feel it's men to whom they have to talk about their boy-friends. 'He's all right. Coo! He'll be wild about the money, lost for good.'

She recovered some of her gushing manner of speech to say goodbye and that she looked forward to seeing us when she came up for the funeral. Jack took her out and the next client was by then so impatient that she followed Jack straight in, and there was no chance to think, let alone talk to each other.

### III

About half past eleven, Jack came back from the waiting-room with his thumbs up.

'Empty at last. Let's go and snatch a coffee.'

'Thank goodness. I'm parched.' We both looked at the empty spot on the desk from which the police had removed the jug and glass. 'I don't know whether I'll ever be able to touch that water again when the police do bring the jug back. Perhaps I'll get a screw-top bottle instead.'

'Good idea, and label it poison. Sorry. I've a perverted

sense of humour. Come on, before another client arrives.'

'I've a phone call to make, Jack. Would you mind going and making the coffee and I'll come as soon as I've finished, even if I have to apologize to a client on the way through.'

I looked up the number of Charing Cross Hospital. A receptionist answered my call quickly, and put me through to Men's Medical without delay, but the nurse who heard my request to speak to Mr Arthur Smithson was away a long time. It was a different, older woman's voice that finally came over the phone.

'Good morning. This is Sister speaking. I understand you wish to speak to Mr Smithson. He is not at all well this morning and doesn't want to speak to anyone. Can I take your name and give him a message? Are you a relative?'

'Could you just tell him now that it's Kit Weatherley on the phone and see if he wants to speak to me. I'd be most grateful.'

I found my heart was thudding so loudly that I was afraid I would not hear the next voice on the line. But I did. And I recognized it, though it was slower and a little harsher perhaps than I remembered it.

'Kit? God Almighty! How did you trace me? Of course, you detect now, don't you? I read all about you in the papers. How's life treating you, Kit?'

So far I had managed nothing but monosyllables, but now I said: 'Pretty well, Ralph. No, better than that: really *very* well. How's it treating you?'

'It's not treating me at all.' The shadow of the old chuckle I knew so well came down the line. 'It's tired of me. I rather suspect it will finish with me completely in two or three weeks. Hell! I never dreamt I'd so enjoy hearing your voice again. Have your looks changed as little? Nice to be able to feel really proud of one's wife.'

'I'm coming over at once to visit you, Ralph. Then you'll be able to judge for—'

'That you are not. Absolutely forbidden. I'll tell the

nurses you are not to be admitted under any circumstances.' The words were strong enough but the voice was not. Listening to it made my own voice weak.

'Why not, Ralph? I wouldn't stay long. I wouldn't tire you.'

'I'm not so sure of that. But in all seriousness, Kit, you are not to come. I'm not going to have you seeing me like this.'

'Ralph, don't be absurd. I've seen lots of ill people. I—'

'It's not just the illness. It's more what these last nine years have done to me. I've had time to notice it lately, and the prospect of dying does wonderfully concentrate the mind, as somebody said. I've had nine years of high living, without any commitments. No family. No need to work. Nothing but the good life. You'd be surprised what that can do for your looks. I'd rather you went on remembering me as you knew me, Kit. Kit? You still there?'

'Of course. I was just wondering if it wouldn't have been better if I'd divorced you straight away after all, let the Chancellor of the Exchequer have the money— it couldn't have hurt him—and saved you from the "good life".'

The ghost of the chuckle came over the phone again. 'I'm glad you haven't changed, Kit. But I don't like that idea. Suppose instead you'd stayed with me. Do you think that might have saved me?'

'Much more likely to have ruined us both.'

This time he laughed out loud. 'How right you are, Kit. But then you always were. I've sometimes thought that's why I let you go. I was scared of the prospect of living with a wife who was always right, especially once she'd discovered how wrong I was.'

'Ralph. I was only twenty-one. I'm not nearly so arrogant now.'

'I don't believe it, Kit. It wouldn't be you. Stop crying, my girl. Pull yourself together and tell me why you tracked me down. Quickly. Sister has started hovering.'

'There's been a man, a junkie, pretending to be you, and he was Arthur Smithson too. I wondered if you knew about it.'

'Don't you worry about him any more, Kit. He's dead, poor bloke. I promise I won't try any more little stunts like that one. Not much time, anyway.'

'I'm not sure that it did end altogether when he died, Ralph. I wondered if you could tell me exactly what was going on and then I could make sure it did stop.'

But it was the Sister's voice that answered. 'Mrs Weatherley? I think that is quite long enough for Mr Smithson to be talking. It is very tiring for him. He must stop now.'

'Can I ring back again later?'

'Certainly not today.'

'Then could I just ask him, Sister, or could you ask him for me, if some time today he could write out a little note explaining what we were talking about and I'd collect it this evening.'

I could just hear her talking to Ralph, with her hand over the mouthpiece no doubt. She came back to me.

'Mr Smithson will write a very short note for you after his rest this afternoon. It will be waiting for you between six and seven this evening at the porter's lodge. Mr Smithson is very insistent that you must on no account try to see him.'

'I promise I won't. Give him my love, please.'

There were a few more words in the background, and then she said: 'He sends you his. Goodbye, Mrs Weatherley.'

IV

I don't know how long afterwards Jack came back to the office, bringing my coffee. I was still sitting at my desk, crying, and trying not to sob out loud because, after all, it was my office, and there might be people in the waiting-room, who were not supposed to know that I could cry. He put the cup down on his own little table, and half sitting on my desk, put his arms round me. He did not say anything or do anything except hold me very tightly, and that was a help because I could let my sobs come out and be smothered against his thick jacket.

After a time, I pulled myself up straighter, pushed him and the damp patch on his jacket away, and found my own handkerchief.

It was not easy to speak, but when I could manage it, I said, between gasps, 'I've been talking to Ralph. He seems to be dying. It's him in Charing Cross Hospital.' I took a few more shuddering breaths and went on, 'He knew about Art and that he's dead. He didn't seem to know that anything had gone on happening since. He's going to write me a note about it this afternoon and I'm to pick it up from the porter about seven. I'm not to see Ralph. I'm sorry to collapse like this.'

'You're doing absolute wonders. It looks as if you've solved it. At seven o'clock we should have all the answers.'

'I'm not sure. I'm not sure he's got them all. And it certainly isn't him who's been trying to kill me or any-body.' I had remembered Jack's ridiculous suggestion the night before.

'Good. That sounds better.' I think he was talking of my condition, rather than of anything I had said. 'Now, what shall we do? How can we smuggle you out through that waiting-room? It's filling up again and it's gone twelve. I'll do what I can with them. You go and have a wash, and I'll get us some lunch as soon as I've finished here. Drink up your coffee first, or is it too cold? Now, come on. I'll make a diversion, while you slip through.'

He certainly made enough noise with his unnecessary enquiries as to who had been waiting longest—the clients sort that out easily themselves. I let myself through into the main house, and went up to my room.

I did not stay there. After looking after myself all these

years, being pampered makes me feel guilty. When I had
scrubbed my face and was once more fit to be seen, I went
down to the kitchen, switched on the fire—I was feeling
cold in spite of the sun outside—and got the soup, rolls
and cheese ready for our lunch. Then, waiting for Jack,
I sat by the fire and thought. I found there was still
another enquiry I might usefully make, and I could not
make it by phone.

When Jack had come in and we were eating, I asked if
he would take the C.A.B. for me that afternoon. 'I really
am exploiting you, and not giving you much training
either. I hope I'll do better next week, when the others
are back. How are you finding it? Easier as it goes on?'

'A lot of the same enquiries keep cropping up, don't
they? As well as some of the same clients. So I think I'm
getting quicker. I'm very willing to do it, but I'm not
happy at your going about on your own, Kate, after that
poisoning yesterday.'

'But, Jack, that could have been meant for anybody.'

'Not really. You're the obvious one.'

'But I can't—anyway, poisoners don't usually use other
methods, do they? Would you like to be appointed my
taster, and I won't eat or drink anything until you've
tasted it? I can't just stop doing anything, Jack. I have
to go on living.'

'I rather badly want you to go on living, Kate.'

He almost made me frightened too. 'I'll be careful.'

'Can't you wait till I can come with you? But, of
course, I'm on our list of suspects.'

I ignored that. 'I really will be careful. I'll get back as
soon as I can. I'm going over to Romford Street.'

'I don't call that being careful.'

'In broad daylight!'

For a moment he said nothing, which I took as acceptance. Then he went on: 'If you must go, Kate, there's
one thing you might do on the way. Call and tell the
police that Ralph is alive.'

'Yes. Yes, that's an idea. But he's calling himself

Smithson and perhaps he doesn't want them to know. I'll
ring them, then I can hang up on them if they ask too
many questions.'

I went into the hall and rang Leman Street.

'Is Inspector Brownfield available . . . No. I won't
keep him long. It's Mrs Weatherley.' He came on the
line quickly after that. 'Good afternoon, Inspector. I
thought perhaps I should let you know that I have discovered my husband's whereabouts. I spoke to him
yesterday . . . No, I'm sorry. He doesn't want anyone to
know where he is at the moment . . . No. But I can reach
him for you if it ever becomes necessary. I hope your
enquiries into the death of Mr Parkinson are progressing.
Goodbye, Inspector.'

'They'll be round here like a swarm of flies, Kate.'

'It was your idea to tell them, and only fair, I think.
Anyway, I'm going out.'

I took my coat and went quickly, before the police
could come.


v


Walking to Romford Street, I wondered whether I was
wasting my time. Once I had collected Ralph's note that
evening, perhaps I would know all the answers, even to
the questions Ralph did not know about. I wished he
would let me see him. Whatever he looked like now, I
would remember him as he'd looked when I was in love
with him. But it would be good to be able to do a little
for him now, after all these years. Perhaps he would
change his mind. I would ring him again in the morning.

I tried to turn my thoughts to the object of this outing,
but instead they turned to Jack. It was with him and
Kevin that I had last walked down here, to the party.
Jack had been wholly a stranger then, and it was not
quite three days ago. Now I felt, not exactly that I knew
him well—he was difficult to know; he fitted no obvious

pattern—but that we were close friends. I'd be glad when
I knew all the answers and could stop holding everybody,
even Jack, in suspicion. It was not easy to hold him there
now.

So back to the questions. Wondering how much of
Lorraine's story had been true, I had thought of one way
of checking her previous truthfulness. If the check were
possible, it might tell me something of Rex and Tim's
truthfulness too. Even when I had Ralph's note, that
knowledge might be useful. But it was a slim chance,
based on my memory of the door of the flat opposite the
squat—probably a squat itself, though with a different
age-group—standing half open as guests went past it to
the party, and of Sheila speaking of the 'old bag' as of a
well-established hazard of life. If some old woman sat
behind that door as permanently and as observantly as
Mrs Weinkopf sat opposite our C.A.B., perhaps I could
discover with certainty who, if anyone, had been in the
flat with Art and Lorraine last Sunday morning.

I went very quietly up the stairs in Romford Street.
Though I would call on Jill and the rest, I would like,
if I could, to speak to the old woman before being absorbed into their company.

On the fifth floor, when at last I reached it, the doors
of both flats, Nos. 12A and 14, were closed. No. 12A had
a bell, but if I rang, would it arouse all the neighbours?
And how would I explain myself to them? But I still felt
I had no time to waste, so I pressed the little luminous
bell-push. The resulting double chime sounded loud to
me on the landing, but I hoped it might not reach much
further. There was no other sound from inside that flat.

I turned to No. 14 and knocked—there was no bell-push.
Rex opened the door wide, holding it open for me to go in
as if I had been expected. Jill, Sheila and Tim were sitting
on their large floor cushions, with a scattering of plates and
mugs around them.

'Good to see you.' Jill could always be relied on to be
welcoming. 'Sorry we're only just finishing our lunch.

Have you had yours?'

'Tim's on a late shift now'—Rex apparently felt the lateness of the meal needed some explanation—'and we all seem to be falling in line with him.'

'Thank you. I think we ate early today. We're fitting lunch in whenever we can escape from the C.A.B., while the others are away.'

'When do they get back?' Sheila seemed more relaxed today.

'Agnes will be back the day after tomorrow, Saturday. Michael and Betty not till late Sunday night, and I don't know about Tom. One never does. That's all there are at the moment, till Eric and Pam get back from Canada, if they do.'

I was feeling surprisingly relaxed too, sitting back and sipping gratefully at the hot coffee Jill had fetched me from the kitchen. But the mood did not have the chance to last long. Tim spoke for the first time:

'We haven't given you Jack's message. He wants you to ring him.'

'He said there was no hurry.' Jill was trying to persuade me to finish my coffee, but I had gone straight to the phone, and with the sketchiest apology, dialled the C.A.B. number. Jack knew I was following the little faint threads I thought might be clues. He wouldn't have told the commune in advance of my coming unless something urgent required me.

He answered at once, 'Spitalfields Advice Centre.'

'I'm told you want me, Jack.'

'Hullo, Kate. You walk quickly. I thought I ought to let you know that I've promised to meet a friend for dinner, after he finishes work. But I won't go out till Kevin comes in.'

'I'll be back before Kevin comes in.'

'I hope so.'

'Then I don't understand. I'll see you then.'

'Yes.'

I hung up, bewildered and beginning to be angry. Was

Jack a fool? He had not so far given that impression. Or was I well justified in keeping him on my list of suspects? Had he chosen to ring in order to give someone in the commune notice of my arrival?

They were all four looking at me. 'He's beginning to behave like a mother hen.' I lowered myself to my cushion and picked up my coffee. 'He thinks we all have to know where all of us are all the time. Or perhaps he thinks it's me is the mother hen—' I was trying to make it sound funny—'and I have to know that he's going out this evening.'

'There'll be Kevin to keep you company.' Tim's jocularity was presumably meant to soothe me.

'There probably won't. He and an old friend meet for dinner every Thursday. But perhaps he won't for a few weeks while his dear friend Jack's here.'

Rex took a turn at trying to soothe me, holding up Jack's better sides to me. 'We all enjoyed hearing Jack tearing strips off those two Marxists the other night. It made a change.'

'Did you see their faces? They're not used to being laughed at.'

'I can't have been looking at them, Sheila. What about you here? Your commune isn't politically inclined?'

Jill answered. 'We seem to have been too busy with individuals like Art, and individual families that need a lot of support. We've been doing what we can for one or two.'

'We're not uninterested,' added Rex. 'We're keen on simple standards, but there's no political party takes much interest in that. That's why we especially appreciated Jack.'

'You *all* want simple standards?'

'Not Lorraine, of course, and poor old Art only in patches. It's Rex and me that are really hooked on them, as the first answer to the world's problems.'

'And our own,' added Rex, in ready support of Jill.

'You never heard Wallie on the subject? He was the

old Warden of Toynbee Hall and he used to go round lecturing on the equal division of the country's resources as the basis of an acceptable life for us all. He reckoned nobody ought to take more than the net average income per head of the country in which they lived.'

'How much is that?' Jill is always practical. But before I could answer, Tim changed the subject. It was interesting that Jill had not mentioned where Tim and Sheila stood on the matter of simple standards.

'Did you meet anyone trying to get into the flat opposite, when you came up here?'

'No.' I was conscious that this was only the thinnest verbal truth. I had not yet thought out how I could justify my unwarrantable interest in flat 12A, without being even less truthful.

'You imagined the bell,' said Sheila, and Jill explained:

'That old woman sits there, behind her open door, most of the hours there are, watching anyone going on up to the next floor or coming in here. It really is too bad she doesn't live on the ground floor where she could see everybody in the block. It's such a waste, seeing only three flats.'

'But Thursday afternoons she goes to a day-centre, so that's the only day her door is shut and the only day her bell rings. And some people'—Sheila was teasing Tim— 'keep thinking they hear it.'

Tim took no notice but turned to me. 'Are the police still badgering you? That old man dying in your waiting-room can't have helped their state of mind. What did he die of?'

'They'll be having an inquest.' My level of truth was very low today. 'It's extraordinary how empty our waiting-room seems without him, even though he hardly spoke.' I hunted for a change of subject. 'How's Lorraine? She's looked in on me and tells me she's leaving almost at once for Margate.'

'Tomorrow, thank the Lord.' Rex had always found Lorraine a trial.

Until Sheila changed the subject yet again, I was wondering whether they knew of Lorraine's claim to be Art's sister. But I thought they would have told me if they had. Or was I not in their confidence? Was I only imagining that a sense of strain had grown in the room, replacing the early sense of relaxation? The feeling could grow from just one person; perhaps it was only my own unease, projected on the rest. So much of my mind was still with Ralph that when Sheila said, 'Tim, why don't you and Kate go together?' I thought for a moment that she had said, 'Kit.' I wonder if anyone else will ever call me Kit.

'Are you going straight home? I'll be leaving for work in half an hour and we could go together.'

If I had not been feeling so cross with Jack, I might have accepted Tim's offer, as part of my promise to take good care of myself. Tim was one person who had had no chance to poison my office water. And the sky was clouding over, which makes for early darkness in February. But I was not frightened, and I was no longer interested in pleasing Jack. I had no wish to spend another half-hour in Romford Street, now I knew there was no chance on a Thursday afternoon of seeing the old woman. I looked at my watch.

'That would have been nice, but I really ought to get back at once. I'm leaving the C.A.B. too much to Jack. Thanks for the coffee. You must all come round again— you too next time, Tim—when the others are back. They'll enjoy meeting you.'

So I walked back on my own, down the busy White-chapel Road. It had been, I decided, a pretty fruitless afternoon.

## VI

I quarrelled with Jack when I got back to the C.A.B. I am not sure why I took out on him my bewilderment at what was happening around me, my anxiety about Ralph and unhappiness that he would not see me, the weight of trying to keep under suspicion all those I was seeing most constantly, and my frustration at the time and energy I had wasted that afternoon. Most probably I was resentful that he now knew so much about my marriage and its break-up, of both of which I am ashamed. One can only be healed by confession if it is made to someone one reveres or loves. I wondered, as I walked home—a very fine drizzle, more mist than rain, was making the dirty pavements slippery—why I had felt so rejuvenated that morning, and the first answer that came to me did nothing to help my current mood.

At a greengrocer's in the Whitechapel Road I bought some fruit for Ralph—our stalls would have packed up long since. But by the time I turned up Commercial Street my thoughts were again so introverted that I would have cut two of my most regular clients, had they not firmly stopped me. I managed, by crossing early to our own side of Wentworth Street, to avoid talking to Mrs Weinkopf, though she shouted across to me, inviting me to join her.

Passing the big window of the C.A.B., I could see that the waiting-room was empty. I found, as I went in through the swing door, that someone had even moved old Sam's chair to stand against the wall, and I stopped to lift it across to the other side of the room. I try to discourage clients—the speechless Sam had not counted—from sitting right beside the fire; it is too near the door of my office, which is far from sound-proof.

Jack looked up from the filing cabinet as I went in. His face brightened so visibly when he saw me that I almost forgot for a moment all I was holding against him. His first words brought it back.

'You're wet, Kate. I can hang on here while you get dry. The police came and went but there have been no clients since the weather turned so nasty, so it's only the phone to answer.'

'Jack—' I moved round the desk and sat in my own

chair, to gain authority perhaps—'you don't have to look after me like this. I've kept myself alive and well for a long time now.'

The happy expression was wiped off his face. 'Sorry, Kate. Most tiresome of me to fuss. I'll hold myself in check.'

'It's more than tiresome. It's damaging to everything I'm trying to do. I go to pay a surprise call on all our suspects in Romford Street, and you find it necessary to ring them up before I arrive so as to make sure I'll know how you're going to spend your evening.'

His silence was so irritating that I burst out, 'What on earth made you do such a stupid thing? The only rational explanation—'

Fortunately he was already speaking as I began that last sentence, so I was able to cut it off. He spoke very quietly.

'I know you refuse to consider yourself in danger, Kate, but whoever put a lethal dose of poison in your water jug shows a degree of malevolence that frightens me badly. When I thought of you walking into that vipers' nest in Romford Street—'

'Your exaggerated language matches your exaggerated fears!'

He shut his mouth tightly for a moment and then went on: 'When I thought of you among all our chief suspects, down in—'

'Other than those in this house.'

'—down in Romford Street, I decided at least I could tell whichever of them happened to be there to receive you that someone here knew where you were and would be looking out for your safe return.'

'Even more like a mother hen than I realized.'

He flushed then, the whole of his face turning a dark red, but it did not stop his mind. 'You were starting to tell me, Kate, what you saw as the only rational explanation of my ringing Romford Street.' I said nothing, so he went on, 'You saw it perhaps as a chance to warn my accomplices.'

We were both silent for so long that I became aware of Mrs Weinkopf, across the road, laughing at some particularly tasty joke. Jack sighed at last and spoke again.

'You're right to think like that, Kate. You've got to go on thinking of me, and Kevin, and everybody involved, as possible suspects. And you've got to protect yourself against us. Look at you now, sitting with me in an empty C.A.B., where I can strangle you any minute. And then I can come in with a cup of tea, and be heart-broken to find you've been murdered by some nasty client. And I'm very persuasive. The police will probably believe me. What are you going to do about it?'

Even that did not move me out of my mood, though by then I wanted to be moved out of it. I would like to have laughed but I could not. I said obstinately, 'I'm not going to give up working, and give up trying to understand what's happening and who killed Sam, and just retreat into a burrow. But it's only for a very little while now, Jack. Once I have Ralph's letter, we should know who is responsible.'

Jack sat and looked at me, as he so often does, before saying, 'It takes only a few seconds to kill someone. It always seems so out of balance with the months it takes to produce a life. So how do you propose to protect yourself these next two hours? I myself find it impossible to suspect Kevin, so once he's home I think you'll be all right. I can collect your note from Charing Cross Hospital on my way to dinner, if you don't mind waiting until about eight-thirty to see it. After that you'll be able to decide—'

'I can decide now, thank you. I am not going to be treated as a baby. I—'

The telephone, which had been surprisingly silent, rang, and three calls in succession gave me only time to fill in the day-book. I had had some chance to recover myself by the time I could turn again to Jack.

'I know you're trying to help me, Jack, at least, I think you're not trying to murder me—' I almost managed a laugh—'but I've so much else I must do, besides protecting myself against a hypothetical murderer. I went to Romford Street to see if the old woman who lives opposite the commune had seen who went in on Sunday morning, so that we'd know if one of them was telling lies. But the one day she goes out is Thursday, so there's that to be done again. And then I've got to see if there's anything I can do for Ralph. So I'll go to the hospital myself for the note, thank you.'

Jack said in a defeated voice, 'I guess you're right as usual, Kate,' and of course he had no clue as to why this apparently harmless statement was as salt on a new, raw wound. The pain nearly choked me. I pushed back my chair and, going to the door, said in an unsteady voice:

'You are never to say that again. I'll leave you to finish the C.A.B.'

I went out through the empty waiting-room, past the empty kitchen and up to my empty room.

## VII

I came downstairs at half past five. I had been lying on my bed, with my little transistor playing fairly loudly to block out the rest of the world. I had never used it for such a purpose before, but it had been entirely effective. I had no idea whether Jack and Kevin were in the house or not.

On the kitchen table I found my bag of fruit—I had left it in the office—and two envelopes, addressed in Jack's small complicated hand, one for me and one for Kevin. So it would seem they were both out. Somehow I had never got round to telling Jack that I did not expect Kevin for supper. And Jack will be telling Kevin to look after me, and me to look after myself, I thought. But I was wrong, about my letter at least. It was brief.

Hope you'll have a useful note from Ralph. If any of his explanations are for the public, I'll look forward to hearing them when I get back from this damned dinner, about 8.30 I expect. Then I'll see if I can make a better go at recognizing your real needs. Sorry to have been so insensitive. Be seeing you. Jack.

In recognition of his having refrained from a single word of caution, and as a token of gratitude for such abstinence, I promised myself I would pay the maximum attention to my safety. While I was in the house, I would open the door to no one but my oldest and closest friends. I wished I had reassured Jack by telling him that the outdoor lock—and that meant the lock of the communicating door from the waiting-room too—had been changed the previous summer, when Agnes had decided that the keys had multiplied undesirably. Now the lock itself was of a most intricate and secure design, and replacements for the eight Residents' keys, or keys for resident guests, had to be obtained from Agnes and accounted for meticulously. It was out of doors that precautions might be more necessary and much more difficult. Were there not old accounts of those in danger of assassination always walking down the middle of the road, clear of the dangerous, lurking shadows? It did not sound very suitable for London. I would at least make a point of staying where there were people and bright lights.

But I had better things to think about, and I wanted to be at the hospital soon after six, even if I had to wait until seven for Ralph's note. So I drank a glass of milk, took my coat and my bag of fruit, and hurried out.

Wentworth Street is almost deserted once the stalls have gone and the shops closed, so I walked defiantly down the middle of it, laughing silently to myself and wishing Jack could see me, until I reached the people and lights of Commercial Street. From Aldgate East I booked to Embankment station, stood well back from the edge of the platform until my own District Line train had drawn up, and made sure of a well-filled carriage. But I could not take it seriously.

Mostly I was thinking of Ralph, wondering what was his illness, how serious it was, when he might agree to see me, what I could take to him. I tore half a sheet of clean notepaper from a letter in my bag, wrote on it 'With my love, Kit' and added our phone number, tucked it in with the fruit and wrote 'Arthur Smithson'—how silly it looked—on the bag.

It was already ten past six when I reached Embankment station, so I ran up Villiers Street—a silly thing to do up so steep a hill. From whatever cause, my heart was pounding by the time I had crossed the Strand and reached the hospital. I did not have to wait. The porter had my envelope waiting in front of him. He accepted the bag of fruit—'It will go straight up in the morning, miss. No, nothing goes up in the evenings'—and even got through to Men's Medical for me.

The soft-voiced nurse wasted no words—she was probably busy. 'There is no change in Mr Smithson's condition. You can ring again in the morning.'

I walked slowly out of the hospital and down into the Strand, the envelope clutched in my hand. I turned into a Lyons, collected a cup of coffee, found an empty table and at last looked at my letter. The envelope was plain buff, not Ralph's style at all; he probably had no stationery with him. It had been addressed in unknown writing to Mrs R. A. Weatherley. Ralph had dictated that all right. I have not used those initials for nine years.

The letter Ralph had written himself, the writing larger than ever but much less firm. The lines scrawled upwards across the pages.

My dear clever detective,
    Here's the rest of the solution you have earned by tracking me down. The sixth substitute for you, my dear Kit, was upset when the doctors not only diagnosed my illness as terminal (what's wrong with the

good old English word fatal?) but also told me when pressed (and pressed pretty hard—how these medicos slide away if they can) that I was unlikely to last to this essential June. (You see, we should have got married in January.) With unexpected cleverness she (or more likely the boy-friend I wasn't supposed to know about, but once I was confined to bed, he was inevitable) discovered a youngish man named Arthur Smithson who had some resemblance to me.

We put in a lot of work on him, getting me dis-charged from one hospital and readmitted to another in his name while he took over my name. The plan was to leave me free to die any time I felt so inclined, leaving the ex-Arthur Smithson, now Ralph Arthur Weatherley, to collect on our tenth anniversary. My girl-friend kept a pretty tight rein on him, lived in the same house, I gather, and seemed convinced that she (or perhaps the boy-friend) could persuade Arthur (a useful noncommittal name) to hand the takings over to them, retaining only a small honorarium. I always thought they might find this more difficult than they expected, but it would by then be none of my business. They were also so foolish as to insist that it would help to palm Arthur off on you. Glad you didn't let me down on that, Kit. Old Pendle's recognition—and he's nearly blind—was all they would have needed. It occurs to me, Kit, that you may well feel that this plan was pretty unfair to you, after you had faithfully kept your promise these nine long years. It was. Perhaps at some unconscious level I wanted to repay you for your righteousness. But consciously I hardly thought of you. It was Death I wanted to beat, Death that thought he could do me out of my fortune. We were going to stop that. It turns out that you can't beat Death. As you know, he has merely made a point of removing Arthur first.

I find I don't mind (though I'm sorry for Arthur of course). At this stage of life, what's a fortune? And I find that I'd rather it went to you than to my clever schemer. Incidentally, as part of our conspiracy I swore by all the gods I don't know that I would never divulge her name (and I still don't know the boy-friend's). I've been passing over the whole of my allowance to her for some months. (This public hospital happens to be better at my particular trouble than any flashy place I might be paying the earth for.) So even allowing for what Arthur was allowed to keep when he collected my monthly money order, the girl has had her whack, and you're not to waste any of your detective skills and softness of heart on trying to trace her and share the fortune. It's yours, Kit. My only fear is that it may buy you another husband as sold on riches as your first. I hope not. I can't give you a reference as a good wife (leaving out those first memorable ten months) but you've been a stalwart business partner. If Sister didn't try to snatch this from me, I might make a pun on mate.

> My Kate
> 's the best bed-mate
> yet though she's sweet
> she's no help-meet
> but a good mate (as in plumber).

How's that?

> Love,
> Ralph.


## VIII

I stood up and left the little table only when it dawned on me that the confusion round me was caused, perhaps deliberately, by a group which hoped for my whole table to prevent their splitting up. I left my full cup of cold coffee. I folded the letter carefully, put it back in the envelope and put that in the pocket of my skirt; obscurely I wanted to keep it close to me.

I was not thinking very clearly and instead of turning back to Villiers Street and the quick Underground, I walked east along the Strand. But awareness of the present grew and when I reached a bus-stop at the same time as a bus, I climbed into it. The conductor who accepted my ten pence smiled at me and told me how far that would take me. I took in the smile but not his words, so only realized belatedly that the bus had turned off the route I wanted, and I had to climb off, and plod the rest of the way home.

I did not even notice the emptiness of Wentworth Street, but I looked hopefully at our house. That was still empty too. All the windows were dark. Even the glass over the hall-door was black, and we always keep the hall lit in the evening when any of us are in.

As soon as I had let myself in, I switched on that light. Then I went down the passage, with the kitchen and then the stairs on my right and the locked door from the waiting-room on my left, and hung my coat on one of the pegs we have fitted across the dead end of the passage. I stood there a moment, looking at nothing so much as the kitchen door, which was very slightly open, and wondering whether, though I had no appetite at all, I ought to go in and make myself eat something. I had had nothing since lunch.

The kitchen door moved, opening a little wider. A hand, in a motoring gauntlet, snaked out of the dark gap, felt up the wall until it touched the switch, and turned off the light.

I did not scream. On the contrary, I stood unmoving in the total blackness, trying not to breathe, trying to silence my thudding heart-beats. But I had not been quiet coming in; the hand knew I was there. It was between me and the outside door. The stairs on my left led only up and up to an end as dead as the corner where I stood. The waiting-room on my right could lead back into the live world—if I could cross it and unbolt the big door, before the hand could reach me—if I could first persuade

my rigid limbs to carry me, silently, to the communicating
door.

The hand was silent, more silent than I.

I tried to test one leg, to discover whether it still had
the power to move. As instantly as if my attempted movement had caused it, there was a click from the kitchen
doorway and the beam of a strong torch shone across the
passage. It swung, unhurrying—it had all the time it
needed—to the outside door, which I—had it indeed been
this same I?—had closed firmly behind me. The light
came slowly back down the passage to explore that communicating door through which I had dreamt of disappearing. Then it moved again down the passage towards me, and my frozen limbs came suddenly to life and
flung me up the stairs on my left.

Noisy as I was, I heard the hand now. It had legs as
well as light and it moved almost as fast as I.

I swung round the first half-landing, by the bathroom
and airing cupboard. Thinking back, I believe I might
have had time to go straight into the bathroom, lock the
door, and climb, screaming, out of the little window. But
I found myself beyond it, on the first full landing, with the
light from a street lamp shining across Agnes's sitting-
room towards me from her open door. I started towards it
—I could lock that door and scream from a front window,
but the torch beam had swung round the turn in the stairs
below me and by some chance shone on the key of Agnes's
door. The key was on the outside of the door; I would
never have time to move it.

I ran—I had not known I could move so fast—up the
next half-flight, swung past the second bathroom—too
high for dropping out of windows, and the back of the
house was unlikely to repay screams—and, up another
half-flight, reached the second floor. I could see the door
of my room, a little open, but the pounding feet were
already rounding the corner and would see where I went,
so I too swung round to go up yet another flight—to the
dead end.

Kevin's door, at the foot of that next flight, was also open—my eyes were now so used to blackness that I could catch the faint outside light through any open door. I had no time to think, but some instinct for survival carried me into Kevin's room even while I wrenched off a shoe and threw it up the next flight. It made a surprisingly convincing noise, as if I had slipped on that upper landing. The light, which had been shining straight into my own room while the heavy feet came up the last flight, swung round and the feet followed it quickly past the half-open door of the room where I crouched, and on up. I gave them half a moment to go round the turn and then, kicking off my remaining shoe, I flung myself down the stairs.

Bathroom landing. Agnes's landing. Those heavy feet could move. They were coming down faster than me. Heavy lorries always gain downhill, I thought inconsequently. Bathroom landing. My stockinged feet slipped on the linoleum, but I caught the stair-rail and swung myself down into the hall. The feet were still on the stairs when I reached the door, opened it—after three years my hand needs no light to go unerringly to the knob of the lock— pulled it shut behind me and was carried by my own impetus down our little dark side road and into Wentworth Street.

I knew I ought to stop then, stop and watch the door of our house to see who, if anyone, came out. I did try. I tried to force myself into the porch of the shop next to Mrs Weinkopf's, the one that sells cloth and that is far enough east to look up the side street, as Mrs Weinkopf cannot. But I had no means of knowing if the feet had already followed me out. That side road is dark but the empty Wentworth Street well enough lit for anyone to have watched me cross the road. Then he could work round to my little dark porch. I ran on until I reached the lights and people of Commercial Street and our door was out of sight.

## IX

My breathing, I found, was making a dry rasping noise.
It was probably that which made the two approaching
women stare at me. The gaze of one stopped at my feet,
though she herself went on, saying as she passed, 'She'll
get chilblains.'

'Nobody gets chilblains now, and anyway it's getting
your feet too hot not—'

The sound of their argument was drowned by the
rumble of the monster lorries that go up and down
Commercial Street day and night. I moved to the side
of the wide pavement before the next passers-by could
comment on my shoelessness. Should I move to the
shadowed spaces under Denning Point, our local tower
block? I could not face shadows. I stayed under the bright
lights, and the walkers who saw me took little notice. We
live in a neighbourhood used to waves of immigrants and
to more than its share of extreme poverty and mental
disturbance. Almost anything goes. The potentially ribald
drunks were still in the pubs, and only one small boy,
hurrying home with his mother, whispered to her as he
pointed to my feet.

But what should I do next? If I walked to anywhere else
in my stockinged feet on the sticky, damp pavements, I
could not hope for the same tolerance. Rationally I knew
this to be wholly unimportant, but my feelings were re-
turning to normal, to our national sense that ridicule is
the fate worse than death.

Some uncounted minutes later, when the traffic lights
at the end of the street had caused a brief break in the
endless stream of lorries, I crossed the road to Toynbee
Hall. Something was taking place in their big old lecture
theatre—I never discovered what. I went in at the public
door, slipped round behind the crowded chairs, and let
myself through into the main building. Toynbee Hall

belongs here: nobody took any notice of my erratic dress
and behaviour.

I sought and finally found the room of one of the
Residents with whom I am slightly acquainted. I was not
ready to tell Don my whole story but he accepted without
comment that I had locked myself out of our Settlement,
and left my shoes and my keys inside. He also accepted
that it was a very long time since I had eaten anything
and left me sitting by his hissing gas fire while he managed
to round up some sandwiches and tea. I had refused his
offer of whisky, and coffee was not mentioned. He appeared as superbly free of natural curiosity as he is of
natural virility and returned happily to his book while I
ate and thought.

I had still to decide what to do next. What I wanted
most was to go home, once Jack and Kevin were there.
I wanted to be warmed in Kevin's kindness. I wanted to
apologize to Jack for not taking his warnings seriously. I
wanted to tell him that Ralph's letter told me only what
we had both already guessed, nothing new. I wanted to
discuss what we might do next to discover what was still
going furtively on, despite Art's death and Ralph's un-
awareness. And I wanted, with some friend, to face and
analyse what had happened to me that evening, in my
home.

But if mine and Kevin's and Jack's were the only keys
in London that could have opened our door that night,
I would do well to go far away, and quickly. I could take
a taxi to Susan's, or I had plenty of other friends nearer
than Susan. I could take a train—Don would borrow
shoes for me from someone in Toynbee—to Nottingham,
and burst in upon the surprised Agnes and Betty and
Michael and Tom. No. Bursting in on almost the last
evening of the conference in my present state would
hardly be good for our Settlement's reputation. I could
see if someone could find me a spare bed in Toynbee.

It was gone nine when at last I asked Don if I could

use the telephone. He led me down to the Residents'
phone, lent me coins—I had left my bag on the little
telephone table in the hall, when I had, a lifetime ago,
hung up my coat—assured himself that I knew the way
back to his room, and left me.

I rang our Settlement number. Jack's voice answered,
quick and harsh as it was not usually. 'Spitalfields Residential Settlement. Who's that?'

'It's me, Jack.'

'My God, Kate, where are you?'

'I'm round at Toynbee. Is Kevin home?'

'We're both home. What in heaven's name—'

'Could you gather up my shoes? I think one is in
Kevin's room and one a bit higher up the stairs. Could
you come round together and meet me, both of you?'

'We'll come round at once.' His voice was lower, more
like himself. 'Is that what you want?'

'Yes, please, Jack. I'll be down on Commercial Street
in two or three minutes.'

They were both waiting in Toynbee's forecourt by the
time I had found my way back to Don's room, thanked
him as adequately as I could—he had given me exactly
what I needed but he is not an easy man to reach, even
with thanks—and he had taken me down and let me out.

Kevin held me steady while I put on the shoes he
handed me.

'Y-you've frightened us h-half-witted, Kate. I h-hadn't
been into my room and found your shoes, or I think we'd
h-have phoned the police. It was bad enough finding
your h-handbag tipped out all over the h-hall table.'

'Was it? Had my keys gone?'

'N-no. Not your keys or your purse or anything
obvious.'

I put my hand into my skirt pocket, and clutched my
letter. It was still there.

'H-have you h-had any supper?'

'Don gave me some, thank you.'

Jack said not a word.

When we were nearly home, I asked, 'When did you two get home?'

'I th-think it was nearly h-half past eight. We met up on the doorstep. Jack h-had come down Cobb Street and I h-had come along Wentworth Street, and we both turned into opposite ends of our little street more or less together. N-neither of us h-had known the other would be out. I h-had quite forgotten Jack didn't know about my regular Thursdays.'

'I ought to have told you, Jack. I was too busy resisting your trying to persuade me to take sensible precautions. Silly of me. I'm sorry.'

He did not have to answer, because we reached our door then, let ourselves in and went together into the kitchen. They had lit the fire and I went over to warm myself by it.

'W-we ought to h-have brought your coat.'

'I'm all right.'

They had put my handbag and its scatter of belongings on the kitchen table. I put them back in the bag.

Jack spoke at last. 'Anything missing?'

'Not that I can see. What he wanted wasn't there.' It was in my hand in my pocket. 'He'll have been looking for Ralph's letter, but it doesn't tell us anything we haven't guessed. Ralph and his last girl-friend and her current boy-friend—Ralph doesn't know who he is—were grooming Art to impersonate Ralph, if he should die before he inherits in June. Then they were going to share out the money. Ralph has sworn not to give away the girl's name, but they must be frightened he might put it in the letter all the same. And in fact, he has slipped up and written that she's living in the same house as Art—as we'd guessed.'

'I-I don't properly understand what you're talking about. But what h-happened tonight, Kate? Wh-who's—?'

'Leave it a minute, Kev. Let's get this other straight first. If Kate doesn't mind, I'll give you the bones of it afterwards. Kate, I know you'll say I'm fussing again, but—'

'I won't. Never again.'

'But you'll have to get Ralph to tell you which of the three the girl is. It's too dangerous not to know. Once they've killed Sam, they can't stop. Why mess about trying to get you convicted of a felony, if they ever were serious about that, which I doubt. Another death would be so much simpler, even safer, and give them the money so much more quickly.'

'I know. I'll ring Ralph in the morning and I think now I may have to tell him what's happening. About tonight—'

I told them about tonight. I could not have wished for a more attentive audience. Even Kevin allowed himself only a few exclamations of horror. Jack was grimly silent, his face growing harder as he listened. When I had finished, he brushed aside Kevin's outpourings of sympathy and said:

'Who could get in?'

'All the reachable windows have those special screws that prevent their being opened more than about nine inches. Agnes has only issued the new double keys to the eight Residents, and occasionally to special long-term visitors, like you, Jack. The makers only supply replacements to Agnes herself, so we're all terribly careful of our keys now. That means that in London at the moment, the only people that should be able to get in—'

'Are the three of us here in this room now. That's why you wanted us both to come together to meet you.'

'That's why.'

We stared at each other stonily until Jack said, 'Who do you trust? Do you trust Susan? Shall we try to get her round tonight to sleep here?'

'She shouldn't leave Harry. It would be absurd.'

'K-Kate, you don't really feel suspicious of Jack and me?'

He was so appalled at the idea that I almost laughed.

'Kevin dear, I don't *feel* in the very least suspicious of either of you. I *feel* you're both people I could trust a long, long way. But I've got to be rational about this. I've let my feelings betray me once too often.' And if Kevin could not understand this, Jack could.

He made no comment on that but said: 'You ought to tell the police, get them to leave someone here tonight.'

'I can't face the police tonight. They've stopped believing anything I say. They wouldn't send round a guard for me. They'll only think I've invented the whole thing, as a diversion. You can't prove I haven't.'

'Let's go together with you to some friend you choose, where you can stay the night. We'll ring Nottingham and get some of the others to come straight back tomorrow morning and they can be with you until Ralph has told you the girl's name and you know who you can't trust and who you can. Then we'll have to go to the police. But let's just get you to a safe bed now.'

'We'll have to ring Agnes now, now it's right inside the Settlement. You ring tonight, Kevin, will you? I've got the phone number up in Agnes's room. But I don't want to go anywhere else. I'll sleep in my own bed. I'll lock my door and put a chair against it.'

'We'll search it first.'

We all went up together, collecting the Nottingham phone number on the way, and when I wanted to stop at the upper bathroom, Jack insisted on looking in that first. They had searched my bedroom by the time I reached it, and chosen a chair for me to fix under the door-handle after I had locked myself in.

'And Kevin and I are both going to sleep on this landing—not that Kevin is likely to wake if I murder you three times over. We're going to search the house thoroughly first, and check all the windows, and Kevin's going to phone Agnes. I hope we won't disturb you.'

'I don't know that I'll sleep very quickly. I'm a bit churned up.'

'I-I've read somewhere that the most soothing thing to think about is money, lots of money, h-how you'll spend it.'

'And you look like having plenty to spend,' said Jack softly, but not at all soothingly. 'Good night, Kate. We'll clear it all up tomorrow.'

# FRIDAY, 18 FEBRUARY

## I

I woke on Friday morning, splendidly hopeful—nothing
to do with money, just the happy sense that today my
sinister opponents could be uncovered. Agnes, I thought
to myself, the utterly strong and dependable Agnes, will
be back and will take over. Maggie will be here looking
after us all. Ralph, when I tell him what's going on, will
tell me who the girl is. And the old woman opposite the
squat should be able to tell me who the man is, and I'll
make myself face it and tell the police, whether it's Kevin
or Jack. But nothing proved so straightforward.

When, in response to their knock and careful duet of
good mornings, I moved the obstructing chair, unlocked
my door, and let in Jack and Kevin with a tray of breakfast, almost the first thing Kevin said was:

'Ag-Agnes and all of them send their love, Kate, and
they're frightfully upset even at the little I h-had time to
tell them. Agnes can't come back till this afternoon. She
h-has to give a talk this morning and the others will be
backing h-her up. She says they h-have written us a long
letter all about the conference wanting this special talk
from h-her, but of course, h-her letter h-hasn't come even
in this morning's post, unless someone's typed the address
and it's one of those two on the tray. But one of them will
come down by the first train this afternoon. So that's
good.'

But it was a disappointment—the first.

I took up my two letters. One was from my brother in
Ghana—good to have, but it could wait. The other, in the
long envelope with the typed address, was the briefest of
notes from Norman and the promised copy of Grandfather
Bloxham's will. I told Jack, and added: 'I can read that

at my leisure. Norman will have told me everything relevant.'

'That reminds me: I've told Kevin the important current aspects of the will. We're both very clear now that if Ralph is not going to live more than a few weeks, the only hope of his inheriting the money and leaving it to the girl is for you to die before then. There's no time to get you convicted of a felony, and once they've killed Sam, accidentally in a sense, holding back from more murders is unimportant. We both see the danger as pretty acute, Kate.'

'After last night, so do I.'

'J-Jack's shown me why we both h-have to count as suspects, Kate. It's h-horrid. I h-hope you'll soon know wh-who are the real villains. Can't the police h-help?'

'I think I'll have to bring them in, but somehow they seem to have me on the wrong side, so I don't expect much. Agnes will sort them out when she gets back.'

'Whoever comes back this afternoon, with a nice, clear record, can be your permanent bodyguard. But we've got to keep you safe till then, Kate. Kevin suggests that he needn't go to work this morning—'

'But Maggie will be here. She'll be a splendid—'

'S-sorry, Kate. We forgot to tell you. Maggie called early to say h-her Cheryl is ill and she'll h-have to stay at h-home. She'll try to make it up some other day.'

So that was the second disappointment.

'I set her mind at rest about Lorraine,' said Jack, and then went back to the business of my protection. 'We're sure you ought not to be left on your own, this side or in the C.A.B. That's not at all a safe place for someone under threat. Can Kevin be any help?'

But I urged Kevin to go to work, assuring him that I would stay with Jack until one of the others arrived, and as Kevin knew it, Jack must be held responsible if anything happened to me. Poor Kevin was still shocked at the suggestion.

When he had gone, Jack said, 'I'm sorry I did not

speak to Agnes too. Kevin is so certain that everything
must be the work of an outsider that he gave Agnes a
most watered-down account. She must be wondering why
on earth you need anyone besides us two strong men. But
someone is coming, and meanwhile, you're my responsibility.'

He might have said it gaily, but he did not. He sounded
grim.

He took my tray away, and when I had dressed, I
went into Agnes's room and phoned the hospital. I was
quickly through to Men's Medical—it helps to deal with
a small hospital—but the nurse who answered did not
connect me to Ralph's bedside; she called the Sister.

'This is Sister speaking. Are you a relative of Mr
Smithson's?'

'I am.' That was still true. 'I am Mrs Kit Weatherley,
and I need to speak to Mr Smithson urgently. I won't
have to keep—'

'I am sorry, Mrs Weatherley, Mr Smithson's condition
is very much worse today. We have been expecting this
collapse for some weeks. He has not been conscious since
early this morning.'

'I'm terribly sorry.' This was a third disappointment,
but that was not why I felt so stricken and hollow. 'Is
there anything at all I can do? I'm sure you're doing
everything that end, but have you addresses of other
relatives?' I remembered at once that it was a silly
question. Ralph was the last of the Bloxham line and
knew nothing of his deserting father's family. To the
best of our knowledge, I was his only living relative. So
far I was still living.

'We had an address for Mrs Smithson, but it seems to
be faulty. Are you in touch with her?'

'No.' But the mention of a Mrs Smithson, a false Mrs
Smithson, brought back my original reason for ringing.
That remained urgent, even through Ralph's worsening
illness. If Ralph was in no position to help me today,
perhaps the Sister could. 'But I might be able to find her,

if you'd just remind me what she looks like.'

'You must be quite out of touch, Mrs Weatherley.' The Sister's voice had sharpened. 'You appear not even to know that poor Mrs Smithson suffered a most disfiguring accident to her face some years ago and never goes out in public without a heavy veil. We tried to persuade her to see if plastic surgery could do anything for her.'

'You saw her face?'

'No one sees her face, as I've just told you, Mrs Weatherley.'

'I see. No, you're right. I don't think I can find her for you. He gave you no other addresses?'

'He wrote a letter yesterday, when he had finished that unnecessarily long one to you, Mrs Weatherley'—it was not only the police I had succeeded in antagonizing—'to some firm of solicitors. But he has given strict instructions that that is only to be delivered to them after his death. No doubt they will be able to find Mrs Smithson, but we should like to have contacted her sooner.'

'Pendle, Son, and Pendle. They'll certainly find his wife.'

'Ah! You do know the solicitors.'

This identification seemed to have softened Sister a little, so I tried a few more words.

'When he is conscious, please give him my love, Kit Weatherley's love, and if he wants to get in touch, or you do, this is my phone number.'

She accepted the number ungraciously—it was clear she would not want to get in touch—and we hung up.

I was still sitting, thinking about Ralph, the old, charming Ralph, whom I had loved and had believed loved me, and who would soon be dead, when Jack came into the room. I had not bothered to close the door this time. He could know I was phoning.

'What is it now, Kate?'

'Ralph's worse. He's unconscious.' But I knew I must not dwell on Ralph and the past. I must think of the present—and try to keep a future. 'And the "Mrs Smithson" who's been visiting him, the girl-friend, I presume, has always worn a veil—she says she's had a disfiguring accident—and gave a false address. So the Sister and nurses can't help us.'

'Have they no other contacts? Is he going to die with nobody and be buried as Arthur Smithson?'

'Ralph has no relations. I don't know about friends. He tended to move about in some current set but he didn't have long-standing friends when I was with him. But the Sister says he wrote a letter yesterday, after mine, to old Pendle. It's not to be delivered while he's alive, but I expect, now Art's dead, he sees no point in keeping up the farce, and he'll be buried as Ralph Weatherley.'

We sat in silence until I looked at my watch and said, 'Time to open the C.A.B.'

'I know. What about the police?'

'I suppose I'd better try telling them about last night. I'll phone now. You go on down and open up.'

'I'm not going to leave you alone in this house after last night. You told Kevin you were going to stay with me.'

'So I did. Sorry. Let's go down and open the C.A.B. and I'll phone the police before seeing any clients.'

As we went downstairs, I said, 'Today's not turning out as well as I'd hoped. But there's still the old woman in Romford Street.'

But somehow I had stopped being hopeful.

II

I had forgotten that the most urgent reason for opening the C.A.B. on time, especially in bad weather, had been to let in old Sam. Today, when we unbolted the big door, there was no one waiting outside. We heard the first client arrive when I was already on the phone to the Leman Street police, but I did not have to keep her long.

The police did not want to take details over the phone.
They were coming round at once to see me.

'They take me more seriously than I'd thought,' I said
to Jack, before he went to call in the first client.

She was an old hand and started as usual, 'I wonder if
you can help me but I don't expect you can. It's been
going on too long now. They don't let up.' The long,
familiar tale of persecution was still in full swing when the
police arrived. I jotted a brief note for Jack, assuring him
the tale need not be taken too seriously—it had indeed
gone on too long—and then took the police, Inspector
Brownfield and a new young constable, through to the
kitchen.

The interview proved as unsatisfactory as I had feared.
The inspector found every aspect unconvincing. He
knew all about our new lock and had the utmost confidence in it. Having asked who had keys and where all
the holders were, he asked if I was accusing Mr Kershaw
or Mr Winters of playing practical jokes on me.

'I'm not accusing anyone. I'm hoping you'll be able
to find who it was, but I don't think it was a practical
joke.'

'Why not? There was no harm done to you, was there?
And there was nothing taken even from the handbag you
say you'd left about.'

My silence on the subject of where I'd been did not
help. I still felt I must respect Ralph's pseudonym until he
dropped it, so I could hardly put the police on to the
second Arthur Smithson.

'I was making a visit in connection with my husband,
whom I've already told you wishes to be left out of this
for the time being.'

I told them I had been in the West End and had taken
a bus part of the way back.

'So you didn't notice the number. Do you usually get
on buses without looking at the number, Mrs Weatherley?
Did you notice the conductor?'

'Yes. I remember he was friendly. He smiled at me

and told me where the bus was going, but I didn't take it in.'

'You didn't take in where the bus was going. And you wouldn't have noticed the conductor's number. Was he a coloured man?'

'Coloured? I don't remember.'

'You don't remember, Mrs Weatherley? You always remember what colour people's eyes are. You said you noticed him.'

'But he wasn't a client. I just noticed he was friendly and smiled at me.'

'Then you're bound to have noticed what race he was.'

'Perhaps I did at the time, but not to remember. I was brought up in Ghana, where we boast about being colour-blind. We notice and remember important things about a person, whether they're friendly and helpful, whether they're efficient, not what colour their skin is.'

'Now, Mrs Weatherley, it doesn't help to get excited. Let's leave the bus and go back to what you did after the incidents you think occurred while you were alone in this house. You went across to Toynbee Hall and went in through the lecture room. Who will have noticed you there?'

'I've no idea. I didn't notice them. But Donald Baker can confirm that I went up to his room, without any shoes or a coat or a handbag, and that he fetched me some food and then lent me the money to phone back here and find if Mr Winters and Mr Kershaw were back.'

'And you told him all about what you thought had happened, about your being chased up and down these stairs of yours?'

'No. I just told him I was locked out.'

'Why didn't you tell him the rest? If all that chasing in the dark had just happened to you, why didn't you tell the very first friend you talked to after it was supposed to have happened?'

'I was shocked and puzzled, and I only wanted to talk about it to people I knew well, who knew all about all the other horrid things that have been happening this week.'

'There was Mr Baker befriending you and you really expect us to believe that if all that had just happened to you, you wouldn't have blurted it all out to him.'

'I don't expect you to believe it.' There are more things in Heaven and earth than are dreamt of in police philosophy.

They gave up at last, without even asking to look over the house, the scene of the aborted crime. I took them out through the waiting-room—another oddity for them to chalk up against me, but I was determinedly trying to keep my promise to Jack and Kevin. There were no clients about. Jack was on the phone when I went back into the office. He turned to me hopefully as soon as he had hung up.

'Were they any help?'

'No. I imagine their first guess is that I'm a sex-starved grass-widow, glimpsing seducers behind every door. Failing that, I'm dragging red herrings across their trail to cover up some dirty work of my own. Perhaps that's even their favourite theory. No wonder women don't report rapists.'

'Up with women's lib!'

'Down with the fuzz!' I was feeling sour.

We went back to the kitchen and gave ourselves coffee. Jack wanted to plan a visit to the old woman in Romford Street during the lunch-hour, instead of waiting for the return of one of the other Residents. His sense of urgency had grown while mine lapsed into a sort of apathy. An awareness of Ralph dying alone in hospital underlay my more active thoughts and reduced to unimportance all our busy-ness.

But if we were to keep actively trying to find solutions for the problems and dangers around us—and it was I who had insisted on this only yesterday—Romford Street, our only remaining line, should be visited as soon as possible. I accepted Jack's arguments and we agreed to go together as soon after one as we could empty the C.A.B.

The waiting-room had filled up again when we went back, and even with Jack answering the phone while I dealt with present clients, it was twenty past one before we could escape.

Jack was bolting the waiting-room's outer door as I went up to the bathroom, but when I came down again, he had come through into the hall and was answering the bell at our own door. It was the police again, four of them this time, a plainclothes man with Inspector Brownfield, and two constables.

For a moment I thought I had been maligning them and they were taking my complaint seriously, but their manner did not encourage such illusions. They pushed past Jack into our narrow hall and somehow elbowed me into the kitchen.

I decided sourness would be a mistake.

'Good afternoon, Inspector Brownfield. How nice to see you and your colleagues again. You have come just at our lunch-hour. Would you all like to share our lunch— just soup and rolls and cheese as a rule, but we haven't made any preparations yet.'

They were much sourer than I had been. Inspector Brownfield did not even answer. The plainclothes detective took charge.

'Mrs Weatherley? And you are Mr Winters? Perhaps we can see you later.'

'Certainly. But I have guaranteed not to leave Mrs Weatherley alone in this house. We believe her to be in danger. So I will just stay in the background here.'

They took it. I would not myself have called being in the same room as four large policemen, one of whom at least was already known to us, as being alone in the house. But Jack has some undefined natural authority and they took it. They ignored him and turned back to me.

'Please sit down, Mrs Weatherley. There are a number of points we must clear up. Did you have lunch here yesterday, as you are planning to do now?'

'Yes. Mr Winters and I.'

'At about the same time as this?'

'Probably a little earlier. We're late today. We have to wait until we have no clients waiting for attention.'

'Would you have the names and addresses of some of the last clients in case we needed them to confirm your timing?'

'I don't understand what this is all about. Certainly I have the names and addresses of my clients.'

'We'll explain in time, Mrs Weatherley. Just a few things we would like to get straight first. Now, when you had finished lunch, you went back into your Citizens' Advice Bureau?'

'No. Mr Winters kindly agreed to take that for me. I had an errand I wanted to do as quickly as possible.'

'Where was that, Mrs Weatherley?'

I considered for a moment whether there was any way my reply might let down Ralph, but decided not; this was the Arthur Smithson they already knew about.

'I went over to Romford Street, where the junkie, Arthur Smithson, lived, you remember, Inspector. I wanted to see the old woman who lives opposite that flat and—'

'You wanted to see Mrs Carmichael?' They were leaning forward in their chairs, the two senior men, gazing at me as if spellbound. 'Why did you want to see Mrs Carmichael?'

'If Mrs Carmichael is the old woman who lives in number twelve A, I wanted to see whether she had been on the look-out as usual last Sunday morning, because of the dispute as to who had seen Arthur Smithson last, Tim Stayner or Rex Mayhew or some stranger. Odd, really, that they hadn't thought of asking her themselves.'

'And what did she say?' They had not taken their eyes

off me, but what was the point of my asking them what was on their minds? They would not answer.

'I never saw her. I rang her bell and no one answered, so I just looked in on number fourteen instead, and they told me she is always out at a day-centre on Thursday afternoons.'

They were sitting back in their seats again. 'And you told the squatters why you were there?'

'No. I was a little embarrassed about my enquiry. After all, it was them I was enquiring about. They were all four there, Jill, Rex, Tim and Sheila—I never remember their surnames. Lorraine is leaving now, as I expect you know.'

'And what are you going to do about Mrs Carmichael now?'

'Mr Winters and I—' I smiled across at Jack, but he did not smile back—'were going to use our lunch-hour going across again to see if we could catch her this time. But if you are still enquiring into anything over there, you'd do it much better than us. Should we leave it to you?'

'We're not going to ask Mrs Carmichael about last Sunday.'

'Then we still will.'

'You'll be wasting your time.'

I realized I was hopelessly at sea. I did not know what was going on. It seemed best to plunge on, saying whatever seemed the most natural thing to say, and hoping light would dawn some time. So I said: 'Oh! Does that mean you know already who she saw on Sunday?' They didn't say a word. 'Or does it mean she didn't see any one? That would be disappointing.'

'It means Mrs Carmichael is dead. Someone went into her flat yesterday and strangled her.'

## III

So the light I had hoped for had dawned, and proved to be darkness. Now we knew what was on the minds of the police, and that our last clue had been taken from us.

Neither we nor the police learnt much more from each other that so-called lunch-time. In reply to their questions I told them when I had left the squat and of my walking back and joining Jack in my office, and of going up to my room to rest before setting out on my unexplained journey to the West End. I did not tell them of my quarrel with Jack. Some hesitation there and about the West End journey made the whole account sound sinister. Even I could see how easily I could fit the role of chief suspect if opportunity was all they looked for. The police appeared to see me as such easy game that they hardly troubled to pursue my hesitations. They could all be opened up in good time.

For once, the police even answered our questions—at this stage, Jack stopped trying to fade into the background. But their replies were more vague, if not as evasive as mine. No one would commit themselves as to exactly what time Mrs Carmichael had left the day-centre. She could have reached her home any time between three, although that was thought to be improbably early, and four-thirty. Her body had not been found until mid-morning today, so the time of death was difficult to fix accurately: between three and eight yesterday evening was as far as the doctors would commit themselves at present.

It was gone half past two when the police went. They left no threats or warnings, but something of them lingered. I expected them every time the door bell or the phone rang all that afternoon.

'In a way, Jack, I *am* responsible for her death, going round making it clear to everyone that she might help us find the person we're looking for. Oh! I wonder if she was old and if she had a family and—'

'Did you make it clear to everyone? You certainly told Kevin and me, and we'd have had lots of time to—'

'I didn't tell the squatters in so many words but some of them had heard me ring her bell and we talked about her seeing everything on that landing. So now there's her, as well as Sam. If I'd drunk the poison myself or not poured it down his throat—'

'What's the time?' I think Jack was primarily concerned with diverting me, and he certainly succeeded. I was appalled to find that I had forgotten the C.A.B., which I should have opened half an hour earlier. Jack tried to take the blame but it was my responsibility. We had had no lunch and if we were to stay together, there seemed no way of getting any. I do not know how we should have resolved that if we had not just then heard a key in the outer lock and each frozen into silence where we stood in the kitchen.

'Katherine will be in the Advice Bureau by now.' I have always loved Agnes's soft Highland tones but on this occasion they had almost reduced me to tears by the time I had torn the kitchen door open and flung myself at Betty. One does not fling oneself at Agnes, but she got the feeling.

She came into the kitchen, drawing off her gloves, and I pulled myself together and introduced Jack to them both. I even had the heart to start organizing again.

'Agnes, I'll try to thank you afterwards for both coming down so quickly. I can't begin to tell you how glad we are. We've felt I ought not to be left alone, because of these attempted murders—'

'And actual murders,' put in Jack.

'So we couldn't see how to open the C.A.B. and give ourselves any lunch. Have you had lunch? Jack can take the C.A.B. on his own.'

I wasn't very coherent, but I had given Agnes enough for her to take over.

'Elizabeth and I had lunch on the train, but we should

be grateful, Elizabeth, if you would prepare something now for these two starving people. If you would be so kind as to take the Advice Bureau, John—' I had never thought of him as John, and it sounded very odd, but Agnes will not abandon her use of the real, old names she loves—'Elizabeth will bring you some rolls and I assure you that one of us will stay with Katherine until we can all be together again.'

Jack took the office key and went at once, managing not only to smile at me at last, but even giving me a sketchy thumbs-up sign. He must have recognized quickly the strength and compassion which underlie Agnes's serene competence—or perhaps Kevin had told him of her.

Betty gave me another hug and then started on the lunch. Agnes turned to me.

'Let us sit in my room, Katherine. I shall be glad of a full account of what has been alarming you all this week.' As we went upstairs, she added, 'If there is nothing you feel should be kept private, we can invite Elizabeth to join us when she brings your lunch. I hope she will take John his first.'

She did, and when she brought up my soup and rolls, she brought coffee for all three of us. She sat by the window, clearly glad to be back home—even without Michael—and let Agnes and me do the talking.

'Let me know if you see the police coming back,' I said to Betty, but they did not yet know of our troubles with the police.

Agnes had started by bringing me up to date on the other Residents' plans. Tom would be back late on Sunday, and characteristically had told no one where he would be between the conference ending this Friday evening and his return. Michael, as soon as the conference ended, would go to his parents as he and Betty had planned to do. They still hoped Betty might be able to join him during the weekend.

I had told Agnes of Ralph, unconscious in Charing

Cross Hospital, of Cheryl's illness keeping Maggie away today, and of Wendy Donovan's pools. We were both, I think, waiting for Betty, and once she was with us, I launched into the relevant happenings of the week.

## IV

I started with the blue-eyed impostor the week before— I had never told them of him—and went on to the dead man in our gutter and our contact with the squatters with whom it turned out he had lived. I did not keep to the order in which we had disentangled that affair. I told them at this stage of Grandfather Bloxham's will and of Ralph's attempt to outwit it, with the sick Ralph and his ex-girl-friend and her boy-friend using Arthur Smithson for this purpose—until his suicide. I told them how our attempts to discover Ralph's allies, from Ralph or the nurses or old Mrs Carmichael, had come to nothing.

Mrs Carmichael's death was a shock to them both, and struck Agnes as meaningless and inexplicable. That was my fault; I had told them of it out of turn. I went back to the will and explained that even when Art's death had ended their hopes of claiming Ralph's money post-humously—and that I believed was all Ralph had ever helped to plan—the money could still be claimed while Ralph was alive, if I were convicted of a felony or died. Agnes's face became very grave as she grasped the implications of that.

I said we thought there had been a very quick, ill-considered attempt, through anonymous information to the police, to implicate me in Art's death. But the post-mortem results had ended that, and if Ralph were as ill as the hospital and Ralph himself suggested, there was in any case no time to get me convicted.

So then there had been the poison in my water, and Sam's death. I don't know what Kevin had told Agnes on the phone, but it had not even included what had

happened to poor old Sam. Betty was especially upset,
and they had to hear all the details before I could go on
to last night's intruder, an intruder who might well have
come straight from strangling the potentially dangerous
witness, Mrs Carmichael. My voice was a little shaky as I
finished.

'I am surprised you did not tell me earlier, Katherine.
You have had an unnerving and dangerous week. Michael
would have come back too had he had any idea of the
gravity of the situation,' she added unnecessarily. I knew
that.

'I thought I had two strong, helpful, dependable supporters. As soon as I realized that I had to count Jack
and Kevin as suspects, I got Kevin to ring you. And we've
been trying to arrange for my safety. Kevin knew that I
was going to stay with Jack the whole of today, until
some of you got back, and we hoped that would make it
too dangerous for Jack, if he is the villain, to attack me.'
In cold blood, it sounded a ridiculously inadequate pre-
caution, but Agnes made no comment. She gave a little
sigh and said: 'Villains. We'd better look at the possi-
bilities, if you are ready to continue, Katherine.'

I said, 'The sooner the better,' and we started on the
list of suspects.

Agnes, and presumably Betty, though she remained
silent except for the occasional question, accepted our
assumption that the original scheme would have involved
keeping a very close hold on Art, who must have had all
the unreliability of a junkie and was yet the key figure,
and that at least one of the two schemers would have
tried to live in the same house with him. Ralph's letter
supported, if it did not irrefutably confirm, this and said
that the girl at least lived in the same house.

'So for the villainess we would appear to have a choice
of only three—' Agnes, as usual, had absorbed all essential
details without apparent effort—'Jill Metcalfe, Sheila and
Lorraine, whose surnames we do not know. Now which of
these must we consider along with particular men?'

'Jill said Sheila and Tim were "a regular couple", and there seems no reason to think otherwise. Except that I remember watching Tim dancing with Jill and wondering if he was a bit attracted there. But Jill is enormously attractive—you ask Kevin—whereas she's never in my presence shown any interest in Tim.'

'And if Jill herself were the villainess?'

'The most obvious boy-friend would be Rex. There seems quite a bit of unacknowledged attraction between them. On the other hand, I suppose she could have something still going with her previous boy-friend, Jim, I think she called him.'

'Or, since she is apparently unattached, with anyone else.'

'You mean, Agnes, particularly with Jack or Kevin? It's rationally possible. It doesn't feel at all right. They'd all have to be such terribly good actors.'

'Just two of them, two extremely villainous schemers.' I had nothing to say, so Agnes went on: 'What can we make of Lorraine? There was apparently something between her and Arthur. Her explanation that she was his sister could have been an imaginative cover story. And I think you said, Katherine, that Rex said Lorraine did not know the difference between fact and fiction. Who could she be teamed with?'

'Not Tim, I think, and Rex always seemed so impatient with her, but I suppose that could be acting again. If Lorraine was the girl-friend then I think the boy-friend is most likely to be someone outside the commune, the one she used to talk about.'

'Could that be John or Kevin?'

'She made eyes at any man. You couldn't tell.' But I had in my mind an ugly picture of Lorraine looking sideways at Jack as she talked about her boy-friend.

'We had better consider who had the opportunity for these attacks and discover whether there are any pairs we can eliminate.'

We looked at opportunity. For the murder of Mrs

Carmichael, no one relevant could be excluded. For the intrusion into our house the previous evening, everyone had to be excluded except Jack and Kevin.

'I will get in touch with the lock-makers.' Agnes looked at her watch. It had gone five. We should have known. Betty had already answered two telephone enquiries. The C.A.B. must have closed. 'That will have to wait until Monday now. They were most warmly recommended and insistent that only they could replace the keys and that the lock could not be forced without leaving signs of the grossest violence.'

'Jack and Kevin checked all round the house after I was in bed last night and found no signs of breaking in anywhere.'

'So until any alternative presents itself, we are obliged to keep them high on our list of suspects.'

'But, Agnes'—this was too much for Betty—'Kevin's a Resident and Jack's one of his oldest friends, even if he isn't after all a cousin and—'

'Elizabeth, our Residents have not proved above such things in the past.' Agnes turned back to me. 'You said that a surprising number of people might have had the opportunity to put poison in your water?'

'Yes. I went to coffee with Jack that day without locking my inner office. I really have no excuse. I've asked Mrs Weinkopf if anyone went in and out during that time and she produced Lorraine, who came back later and again next day and admitted having looked in then. Apart from that, Jack opened up the office for me, and Kevin was with us the previous evening when we showed the squatters round. Tim and Lorraine weren't with them, and Sheila never came into my room. She just stood at the door, right the other side from the jug, and tried to make the others feel they were keeping her waiting.'

We were all quiet until Agnes said, 'As I see it, only Kevin and John had opportunity to commit all three crimes. I am classifying chasing you round the house in the dark as a crime along with the two murders. Jill, Rex and Lorraine had opportunity to commit the other two. Timothy and Sheila could have murdered Mrs Carmichael, but not Samuel, nor been in here last night. We can, I think, eliminate those two. That seems as far as we can get by inductive reasoning, and you, Katherine, suggest that all the outside leads have now failed you. So what should we do? I suggest I should call on the police this evening to clarify their minds and see whether they can help us. I will remember, Katherine'—I had opened my mouth to remind her— 'that at this stage they are to know nothing of Ralph's whereabouts. What else can we do?'

Betty said, 'Perhaps Ralph will be better tomorrow, Kate, and then he'll tell us who the girl is.'

'Yes. And I'll have a long session with Mrs Weinkopf tomorrow, in case she's noticed anything. No. It will have to be Sunday.' All our shops close on Saturday; Sunday is the great day for the stalls and shops in Petticoat Lane. And Mrs Weinkopf, who used to live in a flat above the shop, has moved to where little crippled Bertie can enjoy a garden. The shop and stall do well enough for her to have bought the suburban house she wanted: money has its uses.

'That's Mrs Weinkopf on Sunday and the locksmith on Monday. We're not moving very fast, unless, of course, Ralph can tell us tomorrow.'

'You can still join Michael tomorrow, Elizabeth. I can chaperone Katherine over the weekend. But would you please stay with her now, while I go round to the police. I wish Inspector Wetherby were not on holiday. He knows and trusts us.' He certainly trusts Agnes.

'You can't imagine how wonderful it feels having you both here. Thank you, Agnes. May I just use your phone, and then Betty and I will start getting supper.'

The hospital, when I got through to Men's Medical, said there was no change in Mr Smithson's condition.

## V

The week which had begun so horribly in the cold first light of Monday, with the silent body in our gutter, came to a fearful end on Friday, with crowds and noise and long flames leaping into the red night sky.

We were sitting round the supper table, five of us at last. Agnes's visit to the police had been brief. She had found that her old friend, Inspector Wetherby, was due back next day and she preferred to wait and talk to him. While we ate we were filling each other in on the affairs of our neighbours, or on the Nottingham conference.

'There was so much discussion after Agnes's talk that we never thought we'd catch our train. All the people who still argue that money is the only incentive had—'

Kevin had gone to answer a ring at the street door and half-a-dozen girls rushed past him into our kitchen. Betty's Friday club—it caters for a constantly changing group of young teenage girls, and in theory runs itself— had been safely settled into the waiting-room before we began supper. Having no access to us through the locked communicating door, the girls approach us in their frequent crises by going out into the street, and coming round to our side door.

'There's a fire, miss. Quick, come and see. It's getting a real hold.'

We grabbed our coats from the pegs—it was a blustery night—and pulling the door to behind us, hurried round into Wentworth Street. It was the big warehouse across the road, further west—the one where Tim was working— The one the insurance agent had so rightly been worrying about. The flames we could see were small as yet, but most of the building stretches south down a side street, so we walked together along Wentworth Street until we could see it better.

The fire engines began arriving at the same time, sirens wailing and blue lights flashing. The first two came into

comparatively empty streets, but with the next four came
the crowds. The Fire Service treats any fire here, on the
very edge of the City, with respect. Two engines arrive
within minutes for even a mischievous bonfire on a bombed
site, four or six for anything bigger.

The flames had spread along much of the ground floor
and the wind did not help, but once the firemen were
drenching the worst with hundreds of gallons of water,
some of them died down, to be replaced by billowing
clouds of evil-smelling smoke.

The crowd grew steadily, strangers coming up from
Aldgate High Street and excited youngsters from Toynbee's Curtain Theatre mingling happily with our own
locals. We are zoned as a commercial area, but it is
surprising the numbers that still live here. Their Cockney
calls—'Penny for the Guy'—carried across the hissing of
the water and the crackling of the flames until the
occasion assumed almost an air of carnival.

We met Wendy and Sean Donovan with all five
children, and I almost bumped into Jerry Steel, but he
only talks to those he needs and just now he did not need
me. I was surprised to see Mrs Weinkopf across the road—
I had thought she would have been in her new suburb
long since, but she still feels Spitalfields is her true home.
She was talking to Mrs Goodman and broke off to wave
at me with that air of imperious urgency with which she
seeks to summon listeners. But this was not the time for
the long, exploratory session I planned to have with her,
and in any case, I was sure Agnes would not allow me to
wander on my own.

Strolling down the middle of the road, his arm across
her shoulder, I glimpsed Rex and Jill. I wondered what
had brought them this way, and whether the arm was a
protection or the symbol of a new relationship. But Betty
was dragging me towards Nancy Botcher, an old acquaint-
ance, and I lost them in the crowd.

I was feeling curiously dissociated, and leaving my
safety—most irresponsibly—to the care of the others. The

fire was now belching more smoke than flames, and the busy, ant-like firemen, appearing at upper windows and even briefly peering over the parapet of the roof, seemed like actors in a play. So did the crowd, swaying one moment into the light of Wentworth Street's lamps and then disappearing into the darkness of the little side street, which was lit only by an occasional flickering flame. The firemen kept pushing everyone out of that street; that was where the action was. But the action most real to me was taking place in Charing Cross Hospital.

The voices of the crowd sounded louder as the crackle of the flames lessened, but the hissing water never slackened. One of us—it may have been I—suggested that we might as well finish our supper, and we turned back to the house. We took Jill and Rex, when we ran into them, back with us to share it. I was always glad to see Jill, suspect though she was, and it gave an early opportunity for Agnes and Betty to meet them.

'We started out to see Lorraine off on her train to Margate, and then she suddenly decided she must call in first and say goodbye to Tim.'

'He works at the warehouse that's on fire,' put in Rex.

'But you know that and that he's on nights. He's much too busy with the firemen to talk to us, but Lorraine and Sheila are hanging about trying to see him.'

'What about her luggage?' Betty can be more practical than any of us.

'She's never had much, and she's taking only about a quarter of that in just one big shoulder-bag. She says she'll get the rest when she comes up for the funeral, but she must get to Margate now to tell her sisters about Art.' Jill turned to me reproachfully. 'She says you know she's Art's sister.'

'I've only known since yesterday morning.'

'Why ever didn't you tell us in the afternoon?'

'I wasn't sure that she wanted you to know. I don't know why she told me. And anyway, I wasn't sure it was true. Do you think it is?'

'Yes.' Rex seemed more certain than Jill. 'I know I told you she can't tell the difference between truth and lies, but I don't think she's got enough imagination to invent this.'

'Unless someone put her up to it?' It was an unexpected intervention from Jack.

Rex shook his head. 'Even then I don't think she'd carry it off.'

We had almost finished supper when Rex said almost regretfully, 'Well, that's the end of that little spectacle. I never thought they'd get it under so quickly.'

'You have not lived here long?' We looked at Agnes in some surprise and she smiled and said, 'No. None of you will remember that fire further down this road seven or eight years ago. That was a big warehouse too and said to be doing badly, but they have been very successful in their new premises.'

We sat and waited. This was clearly only the beginning of the story.

'The first six fire-engines controlled the fire quickly. They extinguished all the flames and the firemen went over the whole building, over the roof too, to check that there was nothing smouldering. Then they went home. I was in the Warden's flat at Toynbee Hall that evening and we had a splendid view. It must have been about an hour later that the fire started up again, very oddly, little flickers of flame in many different parts of the building. The fire engines came back, not just six. I counted eighteen at one stage and there may well have been more round the corner. They spurted water in from every angle. They took their hoses on to neighbouring roofs and sent great jets of water into the building. But the flames grew and spread. They were not just crackling, they were roaring. Finally the roof, the roof that the firemen had reassuringly walked over two hours earlier, fell in with a resounding crash, sending great sparks leaping high into the red sky. That was the end.'

It had been so vivid an account that there was a little pause before Rex said, 'So you would advise us to hang about a bit longer?'

Kevin chose to take this seriously. 'B-but the firemen must know now that this might h-happen. They'll wait and see.'

'Why should they? Their job is to put out *existing* fires. They're not paid by the insurance companies.'

'You are a cynic, Jack.' This was from Betty. 'Anyway, let's go out again and see. We've given them nearly an hour.'

Agnes said there were matters she must attend to. Kevin had managed to draw Jill into a private conversation, but Jack and Rex, Betty and I went out again. Betty went into the waiting-room first to bolt the big door—she did not expect her club back—and I stopped a moment to tell Agnes to leave the washing-up. She took the opportunity to remind me to stay closely with Betty. 'The other two are still on our list of suspects, you remember. Are you sure you want to go?'

'I want to be moving. I'll try to remember to stick to Betty. I don't expect she'll forget. Nothing seems at all real to me tonight.'

Agnes is good at knowing what is happening in our minds. She said, 'I do not suppose it would help for me to ring the hospital?'

'No, thank you very much, Agnes. I've bothered them enough for one night.' But she was right in thinking that was what I had been wanting to do, not to ask him any questions, just to learn how he was—quite ridiculous after nine years of not knowing.

## VI

Betty had waited for me at the door—she had not forgotten her responsibilities—and the two men had dawdled along the road until we caught them up. We started together to the warehouse, but Betty and I stopped more often to talk to neighbours, so Jack and Rex were soon well ahead. The fire engines had gone and the crowd had thinned, but there were still little groups of people chatting in the street, hoping perhaps for the flames to leap up again—even if our lives are not so dull as to welcome the excitement of disasters, it is difficult to resist delight in spectacular flames.

I saw Sheila coming towards us—on her own—and had time to murmur to Betty, 'Here's one of the squatters —a non-suspect,' before introducing them.

Sheila was back to not really looking at me, and I had never found her easy to talk to. Betty was no help. After only a few words with Sheila, she said to me, 'I'll just seize this opportunity—' she meant the presence by my side of a non-suspect—'to have a word with Ma Weinkopf. She keeps waving.'

Betty might think me adequately protected; Jack, it seemed, did not. As soon as Betty went from me across the road, he left Rex talking to some friends of his own and joined me. His intentions might have been sinister or benevolent. I had no means of knowing, and somehow did not much care. I was present in not much more than body.

When Betty rejoined us, Sheila said she must find Lorraine and walked away.

Betty, jokingly but unexpectedly, said, 'Off with you, Jack. You're one of the suspects.' She tried to soften it by adding, 'Don't worry. I really will look after her,' but Jack did move away. He had been right in thinking Betty meant it. As soon as he had gone, she said, 'Ma Weinkopf asked me to give you this. It's the people who came to the C.A.B. twice on Wednesday. She says she never can catch you, but she knows you want it, so she's written it down.'

'So we don't have to wait till Sunday.' I looked across the road, caught Mrs Weinkopf's eye and waved at her gratefully. I had no time to look at the paper because this time the long, thin Tim was joining us. He was smudged with smoke, like an old-fashioned sweep—of course, he worked in that warehouse—but he looked stimulated rather than exhausted by whatever he had been doing to put out the fire.

'The other non-suspect,' I muttered to Betty, and introduced them.

Tim hardly noticed Betty. 'I'm so glad to have met you, Kate.' He was as hearty as ever. 'I was just coming to your C.A.B. to look for you. We're having awful trouble with Lorraine. She's locked herself in a loo at the top of the building. I'm in charge of it at night, you know. I'm supposed to put out fires.' He gave me a rather sideways smile and I found myself wondering if he were the one employed to light fires. 'All the big-wigs have gone home now the fire's out, but it's not an easy job tonight, with so many windows wide open to the weather, and looters, and vandals. And now Lorraine. First she said she'd never come out. Then she said she wanted to talk to you first. She's really taken to you. Then when I didn't produce you out of a hat, she started talking about cutting her wrists. I didn't like to leave her.'

We had already crossed the road and started down the side street, beside the warehouse, blacker than ever, with tonight's scorch and smoke marks, but we could not see even those once we had gone a few yards down the unlit, narrow street. The entrance to the warehouse is set right back in a deep alcove, where we were hardly more than dark shadows to each other, but when Tim opened the big door, there was a hurricane lamp just inside and we could at least see each other again.

Tim stopped then and for the first time spoke to Betty. 'Lorraine won't take two people. I'm sorry. She'll think it's some sort of trap.'

'I'll keep quiet.'

'She'll hear your footsteps. In a state like she's in, she's extra sharp.'

'Sorry. I've promised not to leave Kate.'

He stood and looked at Betty, as if there were no urgency at all, and then with a little smile he waved her on up the wide steps that lead from the outer door to the big glass doors that are the real entrance—and that had unexpectedly survived the fire. He stayed beside me, lighting a second hurricane lamp.

It was the smile at Betty which first worried me—not humorous, not friendly, almost wolfish. Belatedly I began to apply a little of my mind to what was going on here, in Spitalfields, and not in Charing Cross Hospital. I did not want to go on into the building with Betty. I wanted time to think first. So I stood beside the lantern and read Mrs Weinkopf's letter—just to gain time. It was scrawled and mis-spelt but not difficult to read:

Dear Missis Wetherly, the once that came twice on Wensday was only too. They came when you was having cofee with the student so did the too that was still wating for you when you come back and theyd not moved from there chairs. The too that come back was the girl what I told you about and the thin man what wurcks at the wearhouse that seed you later. Signed E. Weinkopf.

VII

There had been no one in the little side street with us. The firemen had left a light barrier across the end, and now that nothing was happening, the drifting onlookers preferred to stay on the right side of it, up in the light of Wentworth Street. And Betty was already walking deeper into the dark warehouse.

I called after her, 'Betty.'

It was Tim who answered me. He had lit the second lamp and was now busy bolting the door behind us—to keep out looters—but at least it would need no key to get out. 'She seems in more of a hurry than you.' He smiled pleasantly.

He might be no worse than all our other suspects. His opportunity to put poison in the jug might have been no more used than mine—though had he not in my office implied that his visit was a wholly spontaneous one rather than a second? And the wolfish smile at Betty—was it too late to get Betty away now?

'Mrs Weinkopf has sent a really urgent message. I've only just read it.'

'We must get Lorraine first.' Was it by accident that he stood so firmly between me and the now bolted door?

Betty came back into view at the top of the steps. 'Come on, Kate. Once you're through these glass doors there's a horrid smell of fire about the place. Let's fetch Lorraine quickly and get out.'

I did not know if the two of us could overpower him if we had to. It seemed unlikely. We are neither of us big, nor trained in judo or karate. Nor are we ruthless. Whereas if he were the murderer, he could perhaps hurl one of us against a wall and then catch and deal with the other. The best hope of getting Betty away, since that smile when he had accepted her too, was to show no hint of suspicion.

'Betty, you've said you won't leave me, but as you know, Tim is one of the people we've ruled out from our suspicions, so I ought to be all right with him. And this note from Mrs Weinkopf needs urgent attention. Would you take it straight to Agnes at once?'

Betty was surprised, but she took the paper. She had left me earlier with Sheila, so why not now with Tim? He unbolted the door for her, perhaps a little doubtfully, but he let her go. It was not as though I had written anything on the paper—much as I wished I could. At least this way Betty was safe, and perhaps Jack would read something into my urgency.

Tim was closing the door again when, to my horror, Betty turned back—when I thought she was safe! She ran right back to where we both stood, inside that great empty mausoleum, which smelt of fire, and said: 'Kate, lend me your key. Agnes doesn't always hear the bell and there may be no one else in.'

'Jack can handle the note,' I said, and my mouth felt dry. To distract Tim I added, 'Forgotten your key again, Betty?'

'No, lost it. I can't think what's happened to it. I specially put it into this coat pocket when I was going away'—Betty insists that pockets are safer than hand-bags, and with her perhaps as a rule they are—'and then as it was pouring with rain, I wore my mac instead and forgot all about the key, and it isn't there now. 'Bye.'

Clutching my key as well as the note, she had moved almost out of sight again. I shouted after her, 'That note's in a hurry.' It was my only hope of a lifeline, and I would need a lifeline. I had remembered who had had a chance to go through our pockets in the hall, while the rest of us sat round the table, our supper cooling before us, and Rex saying, 'Where's Sheila now?' I sent a little prayer of apology to Jack and Kevin. They had not had the only keys with which to waylay me last night.

Betty must be safe now, so I could concentrate on trying to save myself, if there was any hope of escape at this stage. Delay was the first essential so I must avoid confrontation. Oddly, Tim would want to avoid it too. So many people knew or would know that I had come with him to this warehouse, 'to help Lorraine', that my death would have to look like an accident.

The door once bolted again, Tim picked up the lantern and urged me on. I moved as slowly as I dared, Tim always close behind me and my shadow swinging grotesquely in front. We went up the front steps and through the glass doors—the smell of the fire was everywhere. We went past the big main staircase, where any searchers would start looking for me—with Tim so close behind me, I could drop no clue—and going to the very back of the building turned up a narrow little stair.

I said, without any conscious plan—Ralph had come

into my mind again, and I found myself wondering if he were already dead, and all this tragic performance to no purpose— 'Did you know, Tim, that I managed to contact my husband, whom poor old Art was impersonating? He's in Charing Cross Hospital and was conscious when I first found him, but he's been sinking fast and has probably gone by now.'

I had turned round on the dark stairs to tell him and we both had stopped. Tim held up the lantern to look closely at my face, to judge, I suppose, whether I was inventing this death. I had not before acknowledged that Ralph might now be dead, and real distress must have shown in my face. Tim lowered the lantern abruptly. But he had too much to lose. He could not afford to change his plans now.

'We must hurry,' he said, and suddenly I feared he was going to swing the heavy lantern at me, so I turned and went on up the silent stairs as if mesmerized, my distorted shadow always before me.

The smell of burning had grown worse as we climbed, but at least the silence was broken abruptly. Feet clattered down the stairs from above us and a lantern swung into view.

Tim stopped. 'Sheila?'

'Yes. It's all—'

'Lorraine's still there?'

'Yes. But it's all going too fast.'

'Get on down. Tell anyone Kate's just getting Lorraine to catch her train.'

She squeezed past, pressing against the wall, as though she did not want to touch me, as though I were already dead. She said to Tim, 'Do hurry,' and ran on down. I found myself hurrying too, and tried to slow down, but Tim was hard on my heels.

After four flights, our staircase ended. We had reached a hall with a window—not opening on the road but on to an inner well, lit by a low, flickering light, a red light, the light of little flames.

I stopped so suddenly that Tim bumped into me, but I hardly noticed.

'Tim'—ridiculously, in face of conflagration, our enmity seemed unimportant— 'we're on fire again. We must get out.'

'Yes. But there's Lorraine first.'

'I don't believe—'

I was going to risk confrontation after all, but Tim had moved to the base of a flight of even narrower stairs and was shouting up them: 'Lorraine! Lorraine!'

Lorraine's voice, distant but unmistakable, came down to us. 'I'm here, you bloody clown.'

I had long stopped believing she was in the building at all.

Could there be three conspirators? Or had I misled myself into deciding that Tim and Sheila were the criminals, and that this was a trap.

'Hell, Kate'—the exclamation seemed wholly appropriate, as the window brightened with a new flame and I heard the beginning of an ominous crackling on the far side of the well— 'we can't hang about. D'you want to leave her to burn?'

I ran up the narrow stairs, Tim close behind me. Lorraine was shouting now. 'Hurry, damn you!'

Tim's lantern behind showed me an open door, from which her voice came, and I ran through it. Three horizontal slits of windows, opening on the well, by now gave enough red light to show that the room I was in was a cloakroom, with basins on one side and lavatories on the other. From one of these Lorraine was shouting.

I did not hear Tim close the door behind me, but I heard the lock turn and swung round, in time to hear his feet running down the stairs on the other side of the locked door.

## VIII

I had walked into this with my eyes wide open. No one
again could taunt me with being always right. But it was
to get Lorraine that I had come up this last flight. I
went to the door on which she was hammering.

'Lorraine! What's keeping you?'

I felt the door, and to my surprise found the locking
device, but it was upside down so I was clumsy opening it.
Someone had turned the door on its head, so that the
little lever with which to lock oneself inside was, instead,
on the outside. Lorraine came out, still swearing.

'You sound all right, Lorraine. Now we've got to get
through this other door.'

She was already tugging at it. Nothing moved.

'We'd better shout.'

Her language was unrepeatable but I understood that
she had long since shouted herself hoarse, and only someone in that ever-brightening well would hear. I looked
for the lock and the hinges, but they were both on the
other side of the door. Tim had chosen his site well.

'We need a battering ram. Can we get one of the loo
doors off?'

I had started struggling with one, quite hopelessly,
when Lorraine said, 'There was a bloody plank in my
bog.'

There was. Tim may have thought he would need it
when changing round the door. I hauled it out and between us, once we'd got the hang of it, we battered the
door. We made some heavy thuds, and the door shook a
little each time—nothing more, but we carried on.

It seemed better not to look at the little window slits,
behind which the flames were growing and now crackling
loudly, but we could not avoid hearing an ominous sound,
as of masonry collapsing somewhere below us—and now
the crackling was below us too.

The plank went suddenly right into and half through

the door, overbalancing us both. We had a long struggle to free the plank again; at least it seemed long to me—I did not know at what pace time was moving.

We were thudding again on the door, a little way from the first jagged slit, when from somewhere above us we heard the shouts. We did not really shout in reply; we both screamed long and loud, pausing only to listen for a reply. It was good when it came. It was a cheerful voice immediately outside our battered door, saying: 'Keep away now. I'm coming in with an axe. And stay low. There's a lot of smoke.'

We crouched at the far end of the room, and the axe came through the door first, and then two firemen and the hot smoke.

They put wet cloths round our faces—they had masks themselves—and bundled us out into the smoke-filled passage, and up some little stairs into clearer air with a window on the street, and a long, long, quivering fireman's ladder against it.

I said, 'She's been in here longest,' and one of the men heaved Lorraine over his shoulder and went out of the window and started down. There were flames at lower windows and the smoke was reaching us now. I could not see very well, nor hear very well. I managed to say: 'There were two other people in the building. Did you find them?'

'There might've been two hundred perishers for all I could count, looking for you in every bloody rat-hole. They've not missed anyone alive. We'd've given up if your people hadn't been so damned sure one of you was here. They never mentioned two. Then we heard you knocking. A good idea, travels further than shouts.'

He must have moved his mask to talk, but the smoke was too much for me and I was only half conscious by the time they shouted up to him and he lifted me over his shoulder and carried me down the long swaying ladder towards the crowd of upturned faces below.

I came to full consciousness again when I heard Lorraine say: 'Hi, Kate. I was just thinking I'd like to thank you. I hope Tim's on his way to hell.'

She was lying on one side of an ambulance and they were lifting me into the other. I struggled. Perhaps I even kicked.

'I never go to hospital unless I'm unconscious.'

In the end, they let me sit up at the back, while they drove me the odd hundred yards to the Settlement.

'You want to go to hospital, Lorraine?'

'You bet. I love being fussed over.'

'I'll make sure Jill knows. We'll all be seeing you.'

When they stopped to let me out—Jill got in instead, to go with Lorraine—I found my legs were not as strong as I had thought. Jack and Kevin—they had all got back to our door nearly as quickly as the ambulance—held me standing until the ambulance was out of sight, and then Jack carried me upstairs. When he was starting up the flight to my room on the second floor, I said: 'We haven't got a fire escape.'

Agnes caught Jack's arm and turned him round. 'Katherine is sleeping on the settee in my sitting-room,' she said, as if that had always been the plan. 'It will be much more convenient for everyone to have only one flight up from the kitchen.'

Betty helped me into my night things, while Agnes made up the bed. Jack brought me a hot drink and Kevin a hot-water bottle. We did not talk much, not even Kevin. They left a shaded lamp burning at my request, but they shut the windows to keep out the smoke and drew the curtains to deaden the roaring of the fire, so I never saw the roof crash in and the great sparks go streaming up to heaven.

## SATURDAY, 19 FEBRUARY

I woke early on Saturday and jumped straight out of bed because I could so strongly smell fire. But it was only the smoke that had seeped in—not until days later, when Maggie had washed all our curtains, were we really clear of it. I pulled back those on Agnes's two windows. The shell of the warehouse stood gaunt, black and roofless. I did not want to look at that.

I stepped back into bed and tried to compose a suitable prayer of gratitude for being alive, but that sort of prayer has to be lived. I thought about Ralph, and I thought about all the Residents and Jack. I thought about the squatters, Tim and Sheila too. I thought about Ralph again, and then I lay and thought at considerable length about money.

It fitted well that when Jack passed my door on his way downstairs, he was singing softly:

'Oh, I could run the Parliament
Or the Courts, I don't care which.
It isn't that I'm lazy, no,
I just don't want to be rich.'

He sounded happy.

I decided it was too early to ring the hospital, so when I had heard all the others go down, I ran upstairs for my dressing-gown, put it on and joined them.

'Good morning, everybody. Betty, why haven't you caught a train to join Michael yet? You don't have to protect me today. I don't have to be suspicious of anyone any more.'

I went round the table and kissed Kevin and Jack in turn to prove it—a most uncharacteristic act on my part, but from their response it appeared acceptable.

'Betty—' they were so pleased with my renewed vitality, that they sat back and let me chatter on—'it's

Sheila who must have taken the key from your coat pocket the night they were here, and then given it to Tim. And she'll have told him there was a water jug on my table. She stood and looked into my office—remember, Kevin? —though she never came in. And goodness, I ought to have taken in all that it meant when she slipped into calling me Kit, that afternoon I went to Romford Street. And if only I'd had the sense to let Mrs Weinkopf tell me about Tim—' I let it go. 'Which of you guessed what I meant by sending you her note?'

They all had. To be told by Betty that I considered the note desperately urgent, to find its only news was to bring Tim back into the list of suspects, and to learn at the same time that I had gone alone with him into the empty, half-burnt warehouse was a crystal-clear message, they assured me—we were all very pleased with each other this morning. They had rushed over immediately, only to find the warehouse again on fire, and the firemen, just arrived back, allowing no one else in. But it was odd that Tim had not met them at the door, with reassuring accounts of having seen Lorraine and me off to the station. Something must have interrupted his plans.

'Did the firemen find Tim and Sheila?'

'No. No one has seen them. Jill has telephoned already this morning. The police want Timothy in connection with the renewed fire, if nothing else. The ruins of the warehouse have yet to be searched, but Rex thinks Timothy and Sheila have probably managed to get over to Greece, as they were preparing to do.'

'B-but surely they can be extradited on a murder charge?'

'If you could prove they'd murdered either Sam or Mrs Carmichael. I couldn't,' I said, and Jack nodded his agreement. 'I hope they stay in Greece.' But I shuddered to think of a lifetime of exile—with Tim, for someone who had been Ralph's girl-friend! 'Do you think it too early to ring the hospital?'

'Wh-why don't you give the night nurses time to go off and h-have someone there wh-who knows all the answers?'

'Jill sent you her love, Katherine, and Rex's. She asked me to tell you that they have rung the London Hospital and Lorraine will be discharged this morning.'

So it was not too early to ring hospitals. I went into the hall and rang the Charing Cross.

I did not need to break the news when I came back—they had overheard enough. It did not seem like news to me. I felt I had known it for a long time.

'He didn't recover consciousness,' I said. 'He died in the evening soon after six.'

They found it difficult to know what to say to someone widowed after nine years of separation.

Agnes said, 'That was a painless way to go, Katherine, and it was good that you had been able to speak to him this last week.'

Betty said, 'Yes, that was wonderful, Kate. That must help.' She came and squeezed my hand.

I looked at Jack and he was looking at me but he said nothing.

Kevin surprised me by saying, 'S-so all last night's h-horror was quite pointless.' That felt unimportant now.

When we had cleared away the breakfast, I went to the phone again, once more leaving the kitchen door open—I was not feeling secretive—and rang Mr Pendle. He is of another generation and so old-fashioned as to think he is lazing if he does not go into the office on Saturday mornings—or perhaps he needs an escape from Mrs Pendle. He answered the telephone himself.

'Kate Weatherley here, Mr Pendle. I hope you and your wife are both well . . . Yes, thank you. You have had no message yet from Charing Cross Hospital? . . . No. You will be sorry to hear that Ralph died yesterday evening . . . Thank you . . . It was not unexpected. He had been ill many months . . . No. I don't know . . . I

managed to find where he was after I phoned you, and I
spoke to him and had a letter from him. He did not wish
me to see him in his present state, so I shall have to ask
you to identify him, please . . . Yes . . . Thank you . . . He
had registered at the hospital under the name of Arthur
Smithson, but as he left a letter for you, I think he must
have intended his real name to be disclosed now . . .
Perhaps on Monday, when you have read the letter, we
can make arrangements for the funeral . . . The death
certificate . . . yes . . . That must be in his own name . . .
Yes . . . Yes . . . The money. I have been thinking about
that . . . Yes, I do understand. Everything still left of his
grandfather's is now due to come to me . . . Yes . . . Very
considerable indeed, yes . . . I have thought about it most
carefully and would be glad if you could arrange for a
quarter of it to go straight to Shelter . . . Yes, for housing
the homeless . . . I have many reasons. I sometimes think
my job would be unnecessary if there were no housing
problem with all its attendant ills . . . Yes. Thank you.
And the other three-quarters to the Charities Aid Fund . . .
Yes . . . Yes. Then I can decide later to what charities
they should pass it on. It is cheating a bit perhaps, but I
haven't had enough time to think it out adequately yet . . .
Yes, of course, Mr Pendle, I appreciate your interest . . .
No. My two nephews are in no sense among the deprived
. . . No . . . No, if I have children, their father and I will
expect to provide for them. I would not wish them to be
burdened with riches . . . Really? . . . I should keep a
very large proportion back to pay capital gains tax? But
surely if it's all going to charities . . . Perhaps you'd be
kind enough just to check that . . . You make it sound
almost as hard to dispose of a fortune as to gain one . . .
Really, Mr Pendle, you'll be telling me next that I can
no longer afford to live in England . . . Yes. Too rich to
afford it. I know . . . Thank you, Mr Pendle . . . I will see
you on Monday.'

When I went back into the kitchen it was Kevin who
this time was silent, almost as though he felt this loss

greater than the first.

Betty, laughing at me, sang, 'Money is the root of all evil.'

Agnes, her beautiful Rs rolling out, said, 'That song repeats an extraordinarily persistent error, Elizabeth. St Paul did not identify money itself as the root of all evils, but the love of money.'

Jack said softly, and yet with an air of congratulation, 'So you've chosen to risk the ditch, Kate.'